Who could Morgan Swift trust?

King, the almost-too-handsome rock star whose pull on her was dangerously strong?

Isis, the platinum-blonde singer-saxophonist who wanted no rivals for King's affections?

Jonathan Swine, the overweight agent who made money his god, and who was willing to sacrifice anything, and anyone, to it?

Randy, the smooth-talking record company wonderkid, who was staking his career on the *Death Trip* videos?

Morgan could be sure of so little. But she did know that her students Sally Jackson and Jenny Wu trusted *her*—and that a mysterious circle of menace was closing around them . . . much too fast!

Morgan Swift
and the
Riddle of The
Sphinx

by Martine Lesley

Random House **New York**

Library of Congress Cataloging-in-Publication Data: Lesley, Mar-
tine. Morgan Swift and the riddle of The Sphinx. SUMMARY: The
adventurous high school teacher accompanies two students to
Egypt to watch a rock group shoot videos, only to find what should
have been a pleasure trip fraught with death threats and terrorism.
[1. Mystery and detective stories. 2. Egypt—Fiction. 3. Rock
groups—Fiction] I. Title. PZ7.L56255Mm 1986 [Fic] 86-47534
ISBN: 0-394-88247-4
Manufactured in the United States of America 1 2 3 4 5 6 7 8 9 0

*To Stephanie, my best friend
and severest critic*
　　　　　　　　　　　—M.L.

Chapter 1

Morgan Swift stirred in her sleep, her body twisting, turning, as if struggling to awaken. But she did not. She was held fast by a dream that both gripped her and chilled her.

She stood under a blinding blue sky on the sands of a vast desert. But though the sun was blazing, an icy wind was blowing, sending shivers through her as it howled in her ears.

Squinting in the sunlight, she gazed up at a mammoth stone statue. It was of a creature with the head of a man and the body of a reclining lion. Behind this awesome figure loomed the vast shape of a pyramid whose point seemed to pierce the sky.

Morgan recognized the statue. It was the Great Sphinx of Egypt. For thousands of years it had humbled all who stood before it. Countless generations had stared up at its face, trying to plumb the wisdom of its all-seeing gaze, trying to understand the mocking irony of its smile. But the message of the Great Sphinx remained as elusive as ever: a riddle as unanswerable as the riddle of life and death itself.

Now, before Morgan's eyes the worn features of the Sphinx grew more distinct, until its face gleamed in the sun as if newly carved. Then the lips of the Sphinx began to move.

Morgan strained to catch the Sphinx's words, as if her very life depended on them.

But all she could hear was the deafening howling of the wind.

If she tried harder, listened more intently, perhaps—

But the wind howled louder.

If only it would die down a moment, if only—

Then the wind was fading.

And the Great Sphinx with it.

There was only the ringing of the telephone.

For a second, Morgan held her eyes shut tight, trying to recapture her dream.

Then she gave up. It was gone.

She opened her eyes and saw that daylight was flooding the room, gleaming on its pure white walls, and emblazoning the three pictures on them: a silk portrait of a smiling goddess from India with a flower in one hand and a sword in the other; a brightly colored poster for a Police rock concert autographed by Sting; and a small oil painting of a strikingly handsome Renaissance prince.

Morgan Swift was back in her world, her time, her place. She was lying under a down comforter on the Japanese mat that served as her bed. She was in her apartment, which occupied the top floor of a Victorian mansion in Langford, the middle-sized Massachusetts city where she taught general science, chemistry, and physics at Coolidge High School.

Almost ten o'clock—missed my morning jog, thought Morgan automatically, before she remembered that a two-foot snowfall the day before had made her usual ten-mile run impossible.

Besides, she had all day to run—at an indoor track. It was a Saturday, and she'd cleared away her work load the night before in a marathon session of grading her students' midterm tests.

Then Morgan remembered she had even more leisure time than that. Midwinter break—a delicious week of February freedom—loomed ahead. Morgan still had no idea how she would spend the time. Perhaps skiing in the north. Or snorkeling in the Caribbean. Or surfing out on the West Coast. Morgan wasn't one for making plans far ahead. Spur-of-the-moment decisions were her style.

For the moment, though, all Morgan was concerned with was how cold her parquet wood floor was as she crossed the room to the ringing telephone. A fresh air fiend, Morgan slept with the radiator off and the window open.

She had to keep her teeth from chattering when she picked up the phone and said, "Hi."

The voice on the other end, however, was warm with joyful excitement.

"We won!"

It was Sally Jackson, one of Morgan's students.

"Congratulations," said Morgan. "Won what?"

3

"The contest."

"The contest?"

"Oh, I forgot. I never told you about it," said Sally. "We felt so silly entering it, and it seemed so ridiculous to think of winning it that I didn't even bother telling you about it."

"Come on, Sally, the *con*test," said Morgan impatiently as she felt her feet begin to turn to ice.

"You ever tune into RTV—you know, music video?" said Sally.

"Does the sun rise in the east?" said Morgan, who had been a rock fan for most of her twenty-four years.

"The contest was on RTV," said Sally. "Maybe you saw it."

"Afraid not," said Morgan. "Things have been pretty hectic the past few weeks, what with figuring out tests to baffle you kids, and then grading them."

"Too bad," said Sally. "If you had seen the contest, I bet you would have entered too. All you had to do was send in a post card with your name on it and you and a friend of your choice could win a trip with a rock group to shoot videos of their newest album."

"And you won?" said Morgan.

"Right!" said Sally.

"Congratulations," said Morgan. "And you don't have to tell me that Jenny is going with you." Morgan was referring to Jenny Wu, who was Sally's best friend, even though the two

4

seemed polar opposites. Sally was the school's head cheerleader and most sought-after date, while Jenny was the class brain who couldn't care less about partying and popularity. The two girls even looked dramatically different. Sally had a blonde all-American beauty and a sense of style that landed her part-time teenage modeling jobs, while Jenny's glossy straight black hair and delicate features would have given her an exotic Oriental loveliness if she ever bothered about her appearance. Which she didn't. Her basic fashion statement consisted of oversize blue jeans and a ponytail.

"Yes—and no," said Sally.

"What do you mean?" asked Morgan.

"We want to go—but our parents have nixed the idea," said Sally. "They don't exactly trust the rock scene, and the place the group is going has had a lot of bad publicity lately. You know, terrorism and stuff. Not to mention unsafe drinking water."

"Parents will be parents," Morgan said. "They do tend to worry about their kids. It goes with the territory."

"I *know*," said Sally. "But imagine missing a chance like *this*."

"Maybe if you and Jenny talked to them," said Morgan. "Promise to stay straight and be careful."

"That's what Jenny and I have been doing for the past eight hours," said Sally. "Jenny's parents and mine won't budge—unless."

"Unless?" said Morgan.

"Unless we have a responsible grownup go with us," said Sally. "We called up RTV and they agreed to foot the bill. It wouldn't help their image to have kids turning down their prize. That's why I'm calling you."

"You're asking me along?" said Morgan.

"It'd be *cool*," said Sally excitedly. "It's over midwinter break, so you won't have to miss any classes. Plus you'd get away from this frigid weather."

"Where is this trip going?" said Morgan.

"Make a guess," said Sally.

Morgan shut her eyes for an instant. In that instant she saw her dream again.

"Egypt," she said.

"How—?" said Sally.

"And the group that's going there is The Sphinx," Morgan said, completing the sequence of deductions that the logical part of her mind clicked off as fast as a computer.

"You cheated," said Sally. "You *have* been watching RTV."

"I guess I must have switched it on for a few minutes and not remembered," said Morgan, who preferred to keep what she saw in her dreams private. Early on in life Morgan had discovered she had powers of the mind that she could not explain even to herself, much less to others.

"Then you'll go," said Sally.

"Egypt *is* one spot on the globe I've missed in

my wanderings," said Morgan. "And there is a lot to learn there about astrology and ancient magic," she added. These were two of her pet interests.

"Then it's yes?" asked Sally.

"Ten-four," said Morgan, grinning.

"We leave Monday morning," Sally said. "That doesn't bother you, does it?" Sally, with Jenny, had been swept up in one or two adventures with Morgan, and she knew how fast Morgan liked to move.

"I'll be ready," said Morgan. "I'll call you tomorrow to work out the details. But right now I have to hang up. I'm standing here in my bare feet on the icy floor—and Twist and Shout have started nipping at my ankles to tell me I'm late for breakfast."

Morgan was referring to her two cats: Twist, a sleek Abyssinian, and Shout, a large, tough, black-and-white alley cat. Both meowed sharply and loudly until Morgan filled their dishes. As they set about devouring the special, low-ash-content cat food that Morgan had determined by chemical and nutrient analysis was best for them, Morgan, on a sudden impulse, went to her television set and snapped on RTV.

She knew what she would see even before the picture appeared:

The Sphinx, the hot new rock group that had sprung from obscurity on the West Coast to the top of the charts in a year with two smash albums.

Their singer was on camera now in a live performance video.

His name was King. He had the six-foot body of a California hunk, a face that quickened millions of female pulses, and long curly brown hair. The way he wore his faded denims had lifted the sale of Levi's across the country. Yet despite the picture of potent power he projected there was something sensitive, something troubled, something vulnerable about his eyes, his mouth. Something that reminded many of the late John Lennon. Something that made his lushly romantic songs even more appealing, giving them depth and resonance.

That special something was coming through in the song he was singing now, stronger than Morgan had ever heard it before:

> *"The sky is empty,*
> *the stars are far away,*
> *the sun is long gone,*
> *I wonder where's the day . . ."*

Not bad—he's really developing, getting his own sound, thought Morgan as she listened to his hard-driving yet plaintive guitar—when suddenly his image faded.

In its place Morgan saw what she would have seen if an x-ray had been turned on King.

She saw a white screen—and in black a picture of a skeleton complete with grinning skull.

It was over in a second. Then the video came

back, showing King waving and grinning to a crowd going wild.

Morgan's mysterious flashes about people never lasted any longer than that. They came like lightning from the unknown. They shed their light on danger. Then they ended, leaving her to deal with the danger on her own.

Morgan snapped off the TV and went to the only source of help she had available at the moment.

Her well-worn deck of tarot cards.

With practiced skill she laid the cards out until she came to the one that would tell her what the trip to come might hold.

Despite herself, she hesitated. The card felt cold and clammy—a coldness that did not come from the temperature of the room.

Then she turned it face up.

Another skeleton, this one bone white, grinned hideously at her. The skeleton was astride a horse and carried a long-handled, evil-looking scythe in the bones of its hands.

The card she had selected was Death.

Chapter 2

Morgan knew better than to be frightened by the card she had turned over. Anyone who knew tarot knew that the card of Death did not signify doom. Instead it meant change, discovery, creativity—the death of the old to make way for the new.

If the card referred to The Sphinx and the new album they were going to video in Egypt, thought Morgan, that might make the trip really interesting. The Sphinx was riding the crest of its first wave of success. Now they had to decide if they wanted to play it safe and repeat themselves or move on. From the song Morgan had just heard from King, it seemed he had already made his decision. She wondered about the rest of the group, especially its female singer, Isis. The last time Morgan had heard her, Isis was still singing about partying all night and buying glittering things all day.

Morgan looked again at the card of Death on the table. Then she thought of the image that had flashed through her mind: King turning into a skeleton.

King was definitely going through changes. But would they turn out to be good or bad for him?

Would they lead to growth?
Or to death?

That question was still in Morgan's mind two days later when she stood face to face with King in The Sphinx's New York hotel suite.

She liked what she saw. King was even more appealing in person than on TV. He was natural, unaffected, even a little shy, almost as if embarrassed by his good looks and talent. He definitely was not into doing the big rock star bit. And the hint of sensitivity in his eyes was even stronger at close range.

It was clear that King found Morgan appealing too. He was polite enough to make sure that his smile of greeting included Sally Jackson and Jenny Wu as well as Morgan when they were introduced, but the two girls could see it was Morgan who interested him. Not that Sally or Jenny minded. Quite the opposite. They would have thought it strange if he weren't attracted to Morgan. In fact, they had been looking forward to his reaction when he saw her.

Five feet nine, long-legged, slim-figured, with strikingly beautiful features and short, punk-style black hair with a startling natural silver streak, Morgan wasn't simply good looking— she was good looking in her own very special way. A way that special people like King were bound to respond to.

"Glad to meet you, Sally, Jenny, Morgan— hope you have a good time on the trip," he said.

11

"Don't believe that hype about rock on the road, though. The day-to-day shooting can be really dull."

Sally broke off from thinking that King had to be the most awesomely handsome man in the universe long enough to say, "I don't think that'll be a problem."

"Right," said Jenny, who was thinking that being bored around King was as likely as two plus two equaling five. "I didn't even bring any books to read."

"Well, I hope we don't disappoint you," said King. "And if things do get slow, I've got a bunch of books on Egypt. It's a real fascinating place. That's why we're doing the video there. It's our first one with a real budget—and I wanted it just right."

That prompted a groan from the man who had met Morgan and the girls at the airport and brought them to the hotel. He was large, not in height but in width. Three hundred pounds at least. All packed into a pin-striped suit with his thick neck bulging out over the collar of a wide-striped blue and white silk shirt adorned with a dark blue silk tie—a perfect outfit for the slender, elegant gentleman he doubtless wanted to be. He was The Sphinx's agent and business manager. His name—and he asked for no jokes when he introduced himself—was Jonathan Swine.

"Of all the places in the world to go—Egypt," he said. "In the Stone Age, electronics-wise. We have to bring in all our own equipment, all our own techies. The costs will be insane, and our contract with the record company says we pay every penny over budget." He shook his head at King. "You used to be such a nice, modest kid. But now you're too big to listen to my advice. You have to have everything your own way. Like the title for this album. It couldn't be like the ones that made you rich and famous. *Bright Eyes. Fire in the Heart.* Oh, no. You have to go ape."

He turned to the girls. "Tell me honestly, kids. Would you buy an album by The Sphinx with a title like this one?"

"But we don't know the title yet," said Sally.

"Though it wouldn't matter—as long as it was The Sphinx," said Jenny.

"Right," said Sally. "We're real fans."

"Thanks," said King with a smile that made the girls' knees turn to water.

"But what *is* the title?" asked Morgan.

"You tell her," Jonathan said to King. "It hurts me even to say it."

King's smile vanished.

"Death Trip," he said.

There was a moment of silence.

"It *is* kind of heavy," King acknowledged, half-apologetically. But his tone grew firm when he went on, "But it's *right*."

Morgan could see there was more than sensitivity beneath King's amazing good looks and natural warmth. There was strength, too. Steel-

13

like strength. It was an interesting mix. Very interesting.

"You're the one who picked the name? Or was it the whole group?" she asked.

"Just me," said King. "My title, my songs. Unless I got them out of my head and out into the world, I couldn't go on to do anything else. That's what I told the rest of the group, and when they understood how important it was to me, they went along—though I guess I didn't give them any choice. It was either that or they had to find themselves another singer."

"You're ruthless, man," said Jonathan Swine, shaking his head.

"Sometimes you have to be ruthless—to do what you have to," said King.

"I'm sure it's a great album," said Sally.

"Absolutely," said Jenny.

"Something important inspire it? Something in your life?" asked Morgan, looking hard at King. Then, with sudden certainty, she said, "A death, maybe?"

"Bull's-eye," said King, returning her gaze. "How did you know?"

"Just a guess," said Morgan.

"My older brother Hal," said King. "Everything to live for—until a drunk driver totaled his car and him."

"Dead—in a car accident?" said Morgan, and for a moment the pain in her eyes linked with the pain in King's. "I know how that feels . . . how it can change things. . . ." Her voice, husky

14

suddenly, trailed off.

Sally and Jenny glanced at each other, then leaned forward to make sure they did not miss anything Morgan might add. In their previous adventures with Morgan,* they had picked up tantalizing hints about a man in Morgan's past, a man named Sam, whose mysterious death had drastically affected her. They very much wanted to know more about it.

"Someone you loved?" asked King softly.

But before Morgan could answer, a voice that managed to be breathless and piercing at the same time interrupted the conversation.

"I'm famished—let's check out room service."

It was Isis, her platinum hair gleaming and a lot of her pale but flawless skin showing through the loose, gauzy white cotton blouse she was wearing with skin-tight black pants.

She had entered from another room in the suite. She was followed by a slight young man whose short, pale blond hair was in sharp contrast to his Japanese new-wave black suit, gray shirt, and black tie. The collar of the oversize suit was worn turned up to frame a face that looked about fifteen years old—unless you looked more closely. Then you saw the fine lines around his pale blue eyes that told you he was at least in his late twenties and maybe even older.

---

*In *Morgan Swift and the Mindmaster* and *Morgan Swift and the Trail of the Jaguar*

There was something else about his eyes that Morgan noticed. A special brightness, like headlights turned way up. This guy was definitely wired, truly hyper, she thought, and Morgan had her thoughts confirmed when she heard the high-intensity brightness in his voice.

"Order anything you want, baby," he told Isis. "It's all in the PR budget, tax deductible."

"Isis, Randy, meet Sally and Jenny—they won that contest to come along with us," said King. "And this is Morgan Swift, their teacher, who's coming too."

"Glad to meet you, girls," Isis said, giving them the kind of automatic smile she would have given a photographer snapping her picture. "And you, too, Morgan," she added, her smile fading. As she sized Morgan up, her hand came to rest on King's shoulder, sending Morgan a message about who had first claim on him. "What do you say to some champagne and caviar, King? This is the life. Nothing but the best."

"That's right, the best for the best—and that's The Sphinx. We haven't met yet—I'm Randy Pike, Megacorp Records," he said, turning to Morgan and the girls. "*Death Trip* is going to be Sphinx's first album on our label. And let me tell you, we're wild about it."

"You're the ones who sponsored the contest," said Sally.

"My idea," said Randy. "This whole album is my baby. I *love* it, and I've made my bosses love it too. They're letting me shoot the works. The sky's the limit on expenses. You kids will have a super time. Starting now. How would *you* like some champagne and caviar?"

"Maybe caviar and Cokes would be better," suggested Morgan. Though she was not strait-laced by any stretch of the imagination, she had made promises to the girls' parents.

"Of course, Ms. Swift," Randy answered instantly. "Sorry about that. I forgot they're minors—they look so grown up. Glad to see you're on your toes looking out for them. Jonathan, call up room service, would you?"

"You're sure it's on your side of the budget?" asked Jonathan.

"You just heard me, didn't you?" Randy replied sharply. "Money, money, money, worry, worry, worry. That's you, Jonathan baby. Don't get me wrong, I think you're a real sweetheart—but you have to learn to think big to make it big. Try it. Think big—big as your suit size."

"I think big—and I think this album and this video is a big mistake," muttered Jonathan. But that didn't stop him from calling room service and ordering caviar and champagne, Cokes for the girls, and a combination lobster and steak platter, complete with baked potato and onion rings, for himself. Before he hung up, he added an order for a double portion of strawberry cheesecake.

"It's going to be a long flight—nearly ten hours—and if there's one thing I can't stand,

17

it's airplane food," he explained.

"What about us field hands—don't we get to chow down too?" said a voice from the doorway. It belonged to a very tall, powerfully built black man with a shaven skull and a full beard. He was wearing a gray sweat suit and black high-top basketball shoes.

"Zack Williams," Sally said to Jenny.

"Keyboards," Jenny said, nodding.

"I could eat a horse," said the very thin young man with spiked silver hair who came into the room behind Zack. The girls recognized him, too. Willie Cohen, percussionist.

"You'll both have to settle for caviar—there'll be plenty for everyone," said Randy.

"If we put a muzzle on Jonathan here," said Zack, giving Jonathan an affectionate tap on the shoulder that made him wince.

"Not funny, Zack, I bruise easily," said Jonathan.

"I figured you couldn't feel a thing under all those layers of good living," said Zack, grinning.

There was a knock on the door and then the door swung open. A wizened hotel attendant wheeled in a cart loaded with covered, silver-plated platters and bottles of champagne in buckets of ice.

"*Bon appétit,*" he said in a very bad French accent. Then he said, "Thanks, man," in a very strong New York accent when Randy slapped a bill in his palm.

"Let me at it," said Jonathan, reaching for

the lid to the nearest platter.

"Hold it," said Randy from the phone where he had just made a call. "Got to wait for the photographer. Got to let the world see the contest winners getting their first taste of the good life."

The photographer, a small man with a large camera, arrived from the room down the hall, where he was staying during The Sphinx's visit to the Big Apple. He posed Jenny and Sally with glasses in their hands and The Sphinx surrounding them in front of the glittering food cart. It was decided to keep Morgan out of the picture, since a chaperone—even one as attractive as Morgan—didn't fit into the image of an RTV dream come true.

"Let's see some real delirious smiles, girls," said the photographer. "Remember, millions of jealous kids are going to see you on their screens tonight."

He took ten shots before he left.

"Finally," said Jonathan, whipping the cover off the largest of the platters. "Hey, what's this?"

An envelope lay across the top of a large bowl of caviar.

"It's addressed to you, King," said Randy. "The fans are sending you mail even with your meals. I've been telling you that you're big— well, let me correct myself. You're not just big, baby, you're *huge*."

King picked up the envelope and opened it. He read it, then said, "Fans, huh? *Some* fans."

"What does it say, that they like me better than you?" said Isis, examining her long silver nails with studied nonchalance.

"Listen to this," said King. " '*Bon voyage.* If you are foolish enough to come to Egypt, your Death Trip will be your own. Your killers are waiting with open tombs.' "

Chapter 3

"Maybe it was the work of a crank—or maybe a terrorist threat," said Inspector Patrick O'Connor of the New York City Police Department, who had come to the hotel after Jonathan Swine's call to report the menacing note. O'Connor was startled to find Morgan Swift, along with Sally and Jenny, on the scene. An old friend and admirer of Morgan's, he had once played a key part in helping her and the girls out of a very dangerous situation.*

"You think there's much danger?" Morgan asked him.

"You never know," O'Connor said. "But it's safe to assume that where there's smoke, there's fire."

"Well, I think there's only hot air," said Randy Pike, heaping caviar on a slice of thin black bread. "Show biz stars attract all kinds of kooks—you can't take them seriously. They're harmless."

"John Lennon would be happy to know that," said O'Connor.

"Look, I don't have time to argue," said Randy. "I've got a show to get on the road. All

---

*In *Morgan Swift and the Mindmaster*

21

the arrangements for the shoot are made. We fall behind schedule, and we lose a fortune. Our plane takes off in three hours."

"Listen, Randy," said Jonathan Swine, "the inspector is right. Why take chances where King is involved? He's too valuable! You're talking about risking millions to save thousands, and you're wrong. Let's just call this whole trip off. And if we were really smart, we'd call the album off, too," he added. "The whole idea is a big drag."

"I hear what you're saying, Jonathan," said Isis sweetly. "And I think it's all too weird for our fans, too. They want us like we've always been—happy, upbeat—not depressing. I mean, why not do a nice video in California with some surf and sun, instead of going halfway across the world to some crazy, godforsaken desert?"

"Can this 'valuable property' put a word in?" asked King quietly. His blue eyes flashed. "I wrote those songs to be heard. Egypt was the place I saw when I wrote them. That's where the videos will be shot. With you—or without you. And if our present fans can only handle sunshine and candy, we'll just have to find new ones."

"What an attitude!" snapped Isis. "Don't tell me you don't care about bombing out. Don't you know that there are a thousand groups out there, just dying to take our place? And have you forgotten what it was like for us a few years ago? Nowhere City!" She snorted. "Well, maybe you don't mind going back there and being Bill Smith, landscape gardener, again but there's no way you'll ever find *me* hustling burgers at a drive-in the way I used to. Iris Jones is history. I'm *Isis* now, a star. And I intend to stay that way."

"King, baby, you've got to remember something," said Jonathan. "This business is crawling with groups that come up fast—and go down fast. You ignore your fans, and you're walking a tightrope without a safety net." He took a huge bite of cheesecake and then waved his fork at King. "Very, very dangerous," he said.

King shrugged. "There's no safety net anywhere, any time, for anyone. I learned that when my brother died."

"Honestly, I don't think I know you anymore," said Isis, putting her hand on his shoulder. "You used to be such a fun person. Now you're so *mor*bid. And so *cold*."

"Not to mention arrogant," said Jonathan. "Maybe the name King has gone to your head. Be careful. You may be riding for a fall."

"Or worse," said Isis. "I don't think the nut who wrote that note was kidding. But at least he was nice enough to give you a warning. Take it."

King shook his head. "If I don't go to Egypt now, I never will. I'll be stuck singing on beaches forever. And I've had it up to here with coconut oil."

"That's right, don't let them scare you, baby," Randy said. "You have to stick your neck out if you want to stay ahead of the pack. Look at me. I'm the one who sold Megacorp on *Death Trip*—despite a lot of folks who said it wasn't bankable. You bomb now, and I'll be right behind you on the unemployment line." He poured himself another glass of champagne.

"Or in the grave," said Jonathan, shaking his head.

"What's the matter, you don't want to go?" Randy said to Jonathan. "Then don't."

"I got to," said Jonathan. "Somebody has to watch out that you don't play games with the books."

"Yeah, we all got to go. We can't afford to miss the exposure," said Isis. Then, as the thought struck her, she turned to Morgan, her eyes narrowing. "Of course, *you* don't have to go, Miss Whatever-your-name-is. You and the kids. I mean, you don't want to lead them into *dan*ger and everything."

"Isis has a point," agreed Randy. "There's really no reason for you and the girls to take risks. Megacorp would understand if you didn't take advantage of our contest offer. In fact, I could arrange a substitute package. A week in Hawaii. Megacorp owns a great beachfront hotel."

Before Morgan could respond, Sally and Jenny gave their answers.

"You wouldn't do that to us, Morgan, would

24

you?" Sally pleaded. "You of all people. Just because of a tiny, tiny risk."

"It's a once-in-a-lifetime chance," said Jenny. "I mean, *you* wouldn't be afraid to do it."

Morgan considered the matter. It was a tough call. She had promised the girls' parents to take care of them. On the other hand, she knew what the trip meant to Sally and Jenny, especially now that they'd met King. And she couldn't help admitting to herself that she wouldn't mind seeing more of him, either. He had so much more below the surface than she had suspected.

"I assume you'll be providing adequate security in Egypt for the group?" she asked Randy.

"The best that money can buy. The Sphinx is a million-dollar investment."

"Do you get threats like this often?" she asked King.

"Me? No," said King. "But I haven't been a big name long. Some others get them all the time. They don't mean much."

"Then I don't see how I can be a wet blanket for the girls," said Morgan. "The most I can do is try to provide some extra security for them myself," she added as Jenny and Sally shot her looks of relief.

"I could have told you Morgan would say that," Inspector O'Connor told Randy. "Take a look at those brown eyes of hers. See the green flecks in them? When Morgan spots a glimmer of adventure up ahead, they start gleaming like emerald chips—just like they're doing now."

Fourteen hours later, Inspector O'Connor was six thousand miles away from Morgan, so he couldn't see her eyes as the jumbo jet touched down at Cairo airport. But he was right—they were gleaming with excitement.

"There's quite a crowd to greet you," the flight attendant said.

The Sphinx party had the first-class section of the plane to themselves. Now they looked out the windows as the plane came to a halt on the runway. They saw a milling, sign-waving mob of people, crammed behind wooden barricades and being held back by armed and helmeted airport security police in black uniforms.

"I heard that American rock was big in Egypt—but nobody told me it was this big," said King.

"Let's face it, we're stars all over the world," said Isis, touching up her makeup before she even showed her face at the window. "Hey, the signs are in English."

"It's the second language here," said Randy.

"There's a sign that says WELCOME SPHINX TO THE LAND OF THE SPHINX," said Jenny.

"And another: KING, YOU'RE THE KING," said Sally.

"Hey, where's my name?" said Isis, squinting hard. Then she said happily, "I think I see it—that sign over to the right with a big *I* on it. Damn, I wish I had my contact lenses in. I can't read what it says."

"I can," said Morgan, following her gaze and

26

feeling a sudden chill. "It says, INFIDELS, GO HOME! ALLAH WILL NOT PROTECT YOU HERE! It's signed, THE EGYPTIAN DEFENSE LEAGUE."

"Infidels?" said Isis, puzzled. "They must have us mixed up with some other group."

"It means non-Muslims," said Morgan. "Not exactly a friendly greeting." She scanned the crowd, trying to spot any dangerous-looking characters, and at the same time trying to quell her uneasiness. There was no sense in putting a damper on the trip for Jenny and Sally until she had something more definite than a vague sense of foreboding, as faint as a distant, barely audible voice. She would just have to make sure she was doubly on guard from this moment on.

"Hey, what *is* this weird stuff?" Isis demanded of Randy. "We got trouble?"

"Not to worry, baby," Randy said. "Just some local crazies. There's a few in every crowd."

"It just takes one to do a number on you—if he has a gun," said Jonathan. "I told you we shouldn't have come here."

"And I told *you*, don't sweat it," said Randy. "We have full government protection, and I've hired even better private guards. Here's the guy in charge now."

An Egyptian had entered the cabin. He was tall, lean, and handsome, and his light brown skin and jet black hair and mustache were in dramatic contrast to his spotless, impeccably tailored white tropical suit.

"Rest assured, you will be perfectly safe in

27

Egypt," he said, flashing them a smile. "I, Abdul Hakim, know how to deal with my more unruly countrymen. We can deplane now."

Morgan was happy to see a group of powerfully built men in suits and ties with shoulder holsters bulging under their jackets, waiting for them at the bottom of the airplane exit ramp. The men formed a flying wedge around them that cut through the crowd as easily as a knife through water. A half hour later, after clearing passport control, they were all in a gleaming minibus, edging their way through the city traffic. This was far harder than cutting through the crowd had been.

"Cairo now has fourteen million people, several million cars, and almost no traffic lights or rules of the road," said Abdul as they looked out the window at a sea of creeping, honking, exhaust-spewing vehicles of all descriptions. Intermingled with the cars and trucks, and adding to the confusion, were horses, mules, camels, and at one crossroad, a herd of goats being shepherded across the street.

"What a scene!" said King. He winced at the chaos of the traffic, the foulness of the air, the deafening noise of motors and horns, and the sight of dilapidated tenements built on rubble-filled fields teeming with ragged children, black-garbed women, and idle men in Arab turbans and robes. Then the people on the sidewalks and in the alleyways disappeared as the minibus passed a seemingly endless stone wall. Rising from behind the wall were rectangular towers and slender minarets. "Why is this part of the city so quiet, so deserted?" asked King.

"This is the City of the Dead," said Abdul. "For hundreds of years people have been building their tombs here. The area covers many square miles in the very heart of the city."

"Brrrr," said Jenny. "Creepy."

"Look—a ghost!" said Sally, pointing at a figure moving out through a doorway in the wall.

"No, a live resident," said Abdul. "Unfortunately, because of the housing shortage, a certain number of the poor have moved into the City of the Dead."

"What a way to live," King said, shaking his head.

"Fortunately," said Abdul with a smile, "*you* don't have to live that way. I think you will find your accommodations superior to this."

"Right. You won't even have to see any more of Cairo," Randy said. "Our hotel is outside the city, practically on top of the pyramids."

An hour later, fighting traffic all the way, the minibus left the main highway and pulled up before a fifteen-story modern hotel. A gleaming glass tower, it was red now in the glow of the setting sun. On the horizon, less than a mile away, were the darkening shapes of the three great pyramids.

"You can forget about Cairo now," said Randy. "It's wonderful what money can do."

"Forget about Cairo?" said King, his hand-some face clouded. "Fourteen million people are a lot to forget."

"I'd like to forget about all of Egypt," said Jonathan. "But if we're here, we might as well enjoy it. I could use a drink."

"I'm gonna check out the hotel shops," said Isis. "I hear Egyptians do great stuff with gold."

"I'm for catching some Z's," said Zack, yawning.

"Sounds cool," said Willie. "Traveling is hard work."

"Good idea, boys," said Randy. "We start shooting first thing tomorrow—and the schedule is rough. You better get some sleep yourself, King. You're carrying quite a load—planning the videos and then performing in them."

"I'm too *up* to sleep," said King. "I want to get into it right away. Where's Brian? He's got everything all set up, right?"

"He should be in his room," said Randy. "He told me last night over the phone that everything's ready—locations, permits, the crew."

"Brian?" said Morgan.

"Brian Dawson—our director," said King.

"He's really good," said Morgan. "But I thought he just did movies."

"He's between jobs—and when I told him my ideas, he got interested," said King.

"What are you going to do—something with ancient Egypt?" asked Sally.

"Any chance we could come along to see you

and Brian work together?" asked Jenny. "I mean, we'd keep our mouths shut."

"Sure, we won't be any—" Sally began to say, only to have a yawn swallow up her words.

"You kids should get some rest," said King. "There'll be plenty to see and do, starting tomorrow. Right, Morgan?"

"Right," Morgan said. "Let's get up to our room, kids."

"Hey, look, Morgan," said King casually, "if you'd like to drop by later and sit in with Brian and me, feel free."

Morgan's eyes met his—and Morgan felt a tremor she hadn't felt in a long time. A *very* long time. So long that she wasn't quite sure how to handle it. Then she got a grip on herself. *Keep cool,* she told herself. *Don't act like a star-struck kid.*

"Thanks," she said. "Maybe I'll take you up on that. But first I want to see Sally and Jenny settled in."

"See you," said King, looking after her as she left with the girls.

Randy had reserved a two-room suite for them. Outside the window were the pyramids, floodlit in the night.

"They really look eerie, sitting out there so close," said Sally.

"They make this hotel seem so small, like a wind could blow it away," said Jenny.

"A wind will be able to blow you away—if you don't get some sleep," said Morgan. "Believe me, those pyramids will still be there when you wake up tomorrow.''

"First I'm going to take a bath," said Sally. "I am totally grotty."

"Don't make it too long," said Jenny. "I'd like one too."

Sally went into the bathroom.

"I hope the hotel has plenty of hot water," Jenny said to Morgan.

"I'm sure it does—it looks like it has every-thing money can buy," said Morgan.

Morgan looked out the window, but what she saw were images of Egypt passing through her mind like images on film. The squalor of Cairo. The glitter of this hotel. The looming, timeless pyramids that looked so close and at the same time so far away. They were like pieces of a puz-zle that fit together—but the picture they formed didn't make sense.

Lost in her thoughts, she dimly heard Jenny's voice.

"You know, I think King really likes you," Jenny was saying.

Morgan tried to think how to answer—when suddenly she didn't have to.

Everything vanished in an earsplitting scream of terror.

Chapter 4

Morgan sprinted across the room and flung open the bathroom door.

Sally, still screaming, was backed against the white tile wall. She pointed toward the bathtub.

A gigantic king cobra snake lay coiled there, its hooded head erect, its forked tongue outthrust.

Instantly Morgan's Swiss army knife was out of her pocket. She flicked out the longest blade. Without seeming to hurry she took aim and then flung the knife blade-first at the snake.

It caught the cobra in the center of its wide throat.

The blade, however, did not sink in. Instead the knife bounced off the cobra as the snake toppled stiffly over on its side after impact.

Morgan walked to the tub. "You can relax, Sally," she said. "It's a fake."

Sally, with Jenny behind her, watched Morgan pick up the snake and hold it up to the light.

"Plastic. Though very realistic," said Morgan.

"I'll say," said Sally. "It was like a horror movie come true."

"But why would anybody play a trick like that?" Jenny wondered.

"Somebody has a truly lousy sense of

humor," said Sally angrily. "As soon as we figure out who did it, I'll give them a piece of my mind."

"I think we may have the answer," said Morgan as she stooped to pick up a piece of paper on the bottom of the tub. It had been lying under the snake.

" 'The ancients of lower Egypt believed the cobra god would protect them against foreign invaders,' " Morgan read. " 'Let this cobra be a warning to you modern invaders of our noble land. Death will strike as swiftly as this snake if you do not go back to America.' It's signed 'The Egyptian Defense League.' "

"Kooks," said Sally.

"Terrorists?" asked Jenny.

"We can find out who they are from Abdul," said Morgan. "But first I want to find out a few things on my own."

Morgan had picked up the piece of paper carefully by its edge. Now she carried it back to her bedroom—one of the two bedrooms in the suite—and laid it on the table. From her large shoulder bag she took the chemistry kit that she always carried with her. First she dusted the paper for fingerprints.

"No luck," she said to Sally and Jenny, who were looking on. "Whoever did this job knew their business. They didn't leave a mark."

Then she took a scraping of the ink in which the note was written. She put it on a slide to examine under her microscope.

"It was a ball-point pen, which tells us nothing," she said. "All I can find out is that the ink hasn't hardened. That means the note must have been written not long before we got to the room. Somebody has a setup in this hotel so that they can move fast and do what they want."

"Yikes," said Sally.

"It is scary," said Jenny.

"That's exactly what it was meant to be—scary," said Morgan. "We'll have to find out from Abdul how real he thinks the threat actually is."

Abdul Hakim definitely thought the threat was real.

He read the note and said, "I was afraid of something like this. The Egyptian Defense League believes that all of Egypt's troubles have come from foreign invaders. First the Persians, then the Greeks and Romans, then the Arabs and Turks, and in modern times, the Western powers. And one of the foreign influences it hates the most is Western popular music. They say it is corrupting and enslaving the nation's youth. The Sphinx is a natural target."

Abdul was telling this to the entire Sphinx group, which had gathered in Randy's suite to confer after Morgan had called him about the threat.

"What a bummer," said Isis. "Let's take the next plane back home. They can have their lousy country."

"I go along with that," said Jonathan. "This whole album is jinxed. Let's cut our losses and cut out."

King shook his head. "Hey, let's not let those creeps scare us. We've got Abdul here for security. And I'm sure the Egyptian government will supply anything else we need."

Abdul shook his head. "Don't report this to the government if you want to stay in the country. They are terrified of such threats. If you are attacked—even if you remain unharmed—the publicity would be ruinous for the tourist industry. That loss is something Egypt cannot afford."

"Hey, baby, no government needed," said Randy. "We got the bucks. You got the men. Put them all together, and those crazies can't touch us. Am I right or am I wrong, Abdul?"

"You're right," said Abdul. "I can assure your safety—especially from the Egyptian Defense League. So far they have shown themselves to be noisy but harmless. They will not be able to penetrate our security shield."

"In case you didn't notice, they already have," said Isis. "It wasn't the good fairy who planted that snake."

Abdul cleared his throat uncomfortably. "It will not happen again. Forewarned is fore-armed."

"Easy for you to say," said Isis. "You're not the ones they're after."

"Yeah," said Jonathan. "And if we leave

Egypt, your paychecks stop."

Abdul drew himself up to his full height. "If you have no confidence in me, I leave this minute."

"Cool it, Abdul," said Randy. "What do you say, King? You're the boss-man."

"The rest of you can do what you want—but I'm going to make this video," said King, his voice firm. "We've got the studio sessions we did on tape, and we can shoot around anyone who isn't here on location. Right, Brian?"

Brian Dawson, a short, bald, bearded man wearing a rumpled tweed jacket and wrinkled chinos, removed a pipe from his mouth and said in a British accent, "We'll intercut shots of the studio sessions with shots of Egypt for all the songs, and we can simply use whatever personnel we have on hand here."

"What do you guys say?" asked King.

"I figure this Egyptian Defense League can't be any hairier than that mob of kids who overran us in Omaha," said Zack. "And I always did want to see the pyramids."

"At least this gig won't be boring—that's the ultimate drag," said Willie.

"You think I'm going to be frozen out of those videos? No way," said Isis.

"I'm not letting The Sphinx get robbed blind," said Jonathan, wiping his sweating pink face with a large handkerchief. "I can't stop you nuts from losing your ratings and maybe your lives on this trip, but I *can* stop you from losing your shirts."

"And maybe *you* losing your ten percent," said Randy.

"Don't you guys ever get tired of sniping at each other?" said King with a grimace. Then he turned to Morgan, his eyes serious. "Look, I'm sorry, we've just been thinking of ourselves. It's the kids and you who got the note."

Morgan's eyes were serious, too, as she returned his gaze. "It's a tough call. One threat in New York, another here . . ."

"But nothing's *hap*pened," said Sally, pleading.

"Nothing *yet*," said Morgan.

"It would be like letting the terrorists have their own way—letting them win," said Jenny, thinking fast.

"That's right," said Sally. "It would just make them stronger."

"It would be practically unpatriotic," said Jenny.

"Well . . ." said Morgan.

"Look, I don't want to influence you, but . . ." said King. Then he paused and grinned. "Actually, I *do* want to influence you. I really like having you people along. It feels good to be with folks outside the business for a change. What I want to say is, come take a look at our first number. It's already on tape. Then decide if you want to hang around to see the rest done. Besides, I'd like to hear what you think of it."

"I can't say no to that," said Morgan, smiling.

"Let's go, before you change your mind," said King.

Morgan and the girls followed King and Brian to Brian's suite. The director had transformed one of his rooms into a workshop, and it was crammed with video cameras, viewers, and editing machines.

"The song is going to be a mix of landscape shots and shots of the group in the studio," said Brian.

"The land around here is a perfect fit for this tune," said King. "Egypt has this ribbon of fertile land along the Nile—and beyond that, total desert. Great dramatic contrasts, which is what the song is about."

Brian turned on a viewing machine. The first scene was The Sphinx in a bare studio. Isis was playing her shining gold saxophone, Zack was on keyboards, Willie played a set of African drums, and King was singing.

From the first chords, Morgan could hear that this album was different from anything the group had done before. Gone was the sweetness, the light, the easy, friendly rhythm. There was a harshness to their sound, a rawness, as if it were being plucked from nerves stretched tight, set to the beat of a heart gone out of control:

> *"Got money to spend,*
> *But it's plastic,*
> *Promises to give,*
> *All elastic;*

Got kisses for you
as fresh as the dew,
But old as the sun
that keeps burning like pain
from a sky
like a wound
that won't heal.
Oh, feel-
ing,
Why am I feel-
ing,
so bad,
so bad,
so sad . . . ?"

Then the sound of the song was repeated, but now on the screen was a scene of tourists splashing in a hotel swimming pool, followed by a flash of Isis on her saxophone:

"Got money to spend . . ."

Then a shot of a vast sea of sand seen from the air:

"But it's plastic . . ."

Then a shot of farmers with oxen plowing a rich field of dark brown earth, followed by a flash of Zack intent on his keyboard:

"Got promises to give . . ."

40

Then a shot of desert dogs—three tiny pup-
pies suckling their mother—in the shadow of a
towering dune:

> *"All elastic . . ."*

Then a shot of Cairo's crowded streets,
jammed with people and vehicles, followed by a
flash of Willie doing an intricate rhythm pattern
on his drums:

> *"Got kisses for you*
> *fresh as the dew . . ."*

Then the lifeless noonday desert, with waves
of dazzling light shimmering up from its surface:

> *"But old as the sun*
> *that keeps burning like pain*
> *from a sky*
> *like a wound that won't heal . . ."*

Then the camera tracked a lone camel with a
cloaked and hooded rider on its back moving
away, growing smaller and smaller, until it was
a speck disappearing over the horizon:

> *"Oh, feel-*
> *ing,*
> *Why am I feel-*
> *ing,*
> *so bad,*

so bad,
so sad . . ."

And that last scene faded into King's face singing the final words, only to have that face fade into the empty desert horizon and silence. Deafening silence.

"Of course, it's only a rough cut," King said. He paused a moment, looking nervous. "But what do you think of it? I mean, it isn't like anything I ever did before. Give it to me straight."

"I think it's sensational," Sally said.

"It sticks with you—it's really strong," agreed Jenny.

"And that last shot—the giant vulture in the sky—is inspired," said Morgan.

Suddenly she realized that all the others were looking at her.

"Vulture?" said King.

And Morgan knew what had happened.

"I was just thinking aloud," she said quickly. "I mean, I was imagining what other touches you could have added. But on second thought, it's perfect the way it is—a vulture would be laying it on too thick."

Morgan alone had seen the giant vulture on the screen. First as a speck in the blue. Then larger and larger. Until the screen was filled with its bloated body, its enormous flapping wings. And then a close-up of its glittering eyes, its ravenous, razor-sharp beak.

She shuddered to think what it might mean.

42

Chapter 5

Morgan stared up at the chipped face of the Great Sphinx. It was exactly as in her dream. But now its lips did not move, and no wind howled. There was only the silence of the desert in the first light of dawn.

"You're not much help, pal," said Morgan. "I'll have to figure out what's going on all by myself."

Morgan had left the others for this private viewing of the Sphinx. Maybe, just maybe, it would provide her with a flash about what was going down on this trip. No luck. Morgan, like so many travelers before her, walked away from the Sphinx with only a sense of how much she as a mere mortal did not know.

She wished she knew more—now that the kids had persuaded her that they should stay on. She hadn't been able to say no to their pleading, especially after that video last night had whetted their appetite for what was to come. Her vision of the vulture, the bad vibes she sensed getting stronger and stronger, even the messages of menace they had received, weren't convincing enough to make her want to kill their chance for an experience of a lifetime—and, to tell the truth, her own chance of finding out what was

43

behind it all. Once Morgan had heard a replay of a radio program popular before she was born. *I Love a Mystery* it was called, and Morgan knew just what it meant—though she also knew how dangerous her permanent love affair with the unknown could be.

She was willing to run the risk, take the weight—but from now on in Egypt, she couldn't relax her vigilance over the kids for a moment. She'd trust no one, and be on guard for anything.

Against a sky that was turning from dark purple to pale blue, she viewed the three Giza pyramids a few hundred feet away: the Great Pyramid of King Cheops and, in diminishing size, the pyramids of his son and grandson. Once they had been covered in smooth alabaster, but that alabaster had been stripped away by countless generations of looters. No longer were the pyramids images of eternal godlike perfection. Instead they presented a breathtaking picture of huge, time-worn blocks of granite fitted together to form giant stepping stones to the sky.

Morgan rejoined Sally and Jenny at the foot of the Great Pyramid.

King was staring at it, spellbound.

"Those old kings had conquered everything around them on earth," he said. "And they figured they should be able to conquer death, too. So they put all their money and power into something that could last for all time and protect them forever." He shook his head. "I've been reading up on their religion. Seems they believed that everybody had this spirit twin that was created with them and didn't die. The Ka, they called it. And as long as their body stayed intact after death, even as long as pictures or statues of them existed, their Ka would have a home, and not have to wander in empty air. These kings wanted to preserve their bodies forever—that's why they were so big on being turned into mummies after death. They even had pictures of their officials, soldiers, and servants in their tombs, so that the Kas of all those people could serve them forever. Those guys really thought they could beat out death and take it all with them." King smiled a crooked smile. "Fat chance."

Morgan and the girls stood there in silence. Then Brian Dawson's voice brought them sharply back to the present.

"Let's get this show on the road!" shouted Brian. "We only have a few hours to shoot before the tourists get here."

The group emerged from the minibus, dressed for the video. Zack and Willie were dressed as King was, in gray three-piece Brooks Brothers suits, white shirts, and navy and white polka-dot ties. Isis was dressed in the Yuppie woman's version of the suit, complete with floppy paisley bow tie, horn-rimmed glasses, and running shoes.

"This is totally crazy," said Isis. "It'll totally

45

wreck my image—not to mention my skin!"

"Time's a-wasting. Up you go, my girl," said Brian, boosting her up onto the first row of stone blocks of the pyramid. "You should be grateful we have government permission to climb up this thing. Tourists are forbidden to, you know. Too dangerous."

"Lucky us," said Isis with a grimace as she strained to mount the second row of blocks.

Meanwhile the others were climbing up the side of the pyramid too. As they groped for handholds and footholds, they were filmed by camera operators stationed above them, below them, and climbing with them. Morgan could imagine how it would appear on the video screen after the filming and editing. There would be long shots of their bodies tiny against the sloping side of the pyramid, and close-ups of their grasping hands and grimacing faces with sweat beading their skin and dripping onto their suits as the sun and the temperature rose. It was the perfect image of a desperate struggle upward.

Watching it, Morgan felt an irrepressible urge to try the climb herself. "I'm going up," she told Sally and Jenny. "Stay with the crew, okay? I'll be down soon." She led the girls to the side of the pyramid away from the cameras. As she started up she said, "You don't mind if I go on alone, do you? This climb isn't for beginners."

"We don't mind at all," Sally told her.

"Right, don't let us cramp your style," agreed

Jenny. Sometimes Morgan's energy was a little bit overwhelming.

"See you in a while," said Morgan. She set out, and soon felt the pleasure of forgetting everything in pure physical effort. She hadn't rock-climbed in years, and had almost forgotten the fun of going up and up, winning out over all obstacles to reach a peak.

From below her she heard the tape Brian was playing over a loudspeaker to set the rhythm and convey the meaning of the climb scene. King's voice had a harsh, cutting edge of mocking irony as he sang:

"Climbing high,
climbing high,
climbing high,
it's to die,
it's to die,
it's to die.

See the sky,
see the sky,
see the sky,
it's to die,
it's to die,
it's to die.

Gonna fly,
gonna fly,
gonna fly,
it's to die,
it's to die,
it's to die.

47

> *Don't cry,*
> *don't cry,*
> *don't cry,*
> *it's to die,*
> *it's to die,*
> *it's to die."*

Nice idea—all those eager-beaver Yuppie climbers, thinking all they have to worry about is getting ahead, thought Morgan as the song grew fainter and fainter. Then it faded from her mind and she lost all sense of time as she went higher. Soon all she knew was the shape and feel of the stone beneath her hands and feet and her muscles stretching to their limit. Finally all she knew was the dizzying exhilaration of reaching the top. Her breath burning in her lungs, she was about to turn her head to enjoy the view when she heard King's voice, startlingly close:

"Hey, fancy meeting you here." He was barely two feet away.

"I couldn't resist it," he said. "Once you start climbing, it's hard to stop."

"Hey, you're in good shape," said Morgan. "It's quite a climb."

"You're in pretty good shape yourself," said King.

Their eyes met, and Morgan felt something electric pass between them. Standing on top of the pyramid, her foothold was secure; but for one brief moment she felt as if she might be losing her balance.

Then almost instantly she was back in command of herself and her emotions. "Let's see what we can see," she said, and swept the horizon with her high-powered field glasses. On one side she saw the empty white sand stretching to meet the blue of the sky; on the other, Cairo, under a gray cloud of pollution.

"Quite a view," she said to King, handing him the glasses.

"Sure is," he said. Then he pointed the glasses downward and said, "This is what a god must feel like—looking down and seeing people who can't see you. Take a look."

He passed the glasses back to Morgan. The group had climbed down from the pyramid. Isis's mascara was smeared with sweat and her eyes were angry as she spoke to Brian, doubtless telling him just what she thought of this video. Willie, his spiked hair wilted, was chugalugging a bottle of soda. Then Morgan focused on Zack, and her hands tightened on the glasses.

First he was tottering, and then he fell. As the crew watched, shocked, he hit the ground and then lay there, doubled over in pain. Then they gathered around him, and he was blocked from view.

"Come on," Morgan said to King. "Our time for playing god is over. It's time to get back to earth."

Chapter 6

Morgan may have lost all sense of time climbing up the pyramid, but she was all too agonizingly aware of how long it took her to climb down. It seemed like forever. By the time she and King reached the ground, Zack had been driven away to the nearest hospital.

"He got these terrific pains in his stomach," said Willie. "He said they were like knives. One of the tourists waiting to come in was a doctor. He thought Zack had picked up some Egyptian bug in the food or water—it happens to a lot of foreigners here."

"Egyptian bug—this whole trip is buggy," said Isis.

"The sooner we get out of here the better," said Jonathan. "It's bad enough this album is going to kill our future—this video is going to wind up killing us."

"I say we pack it in," said Isis. "Let's take a vote, here and now."

In answer, King looked at his watch. "We've got another video to shoot in an hour," he said quietly. "Whether Zack is sick or not, we've got to stick to schedule. Look, Isis, you're not in this next video. Why not go back to the hotel and decide whether you want to stick around or just go back home? Nobody's holding you here against your will."

He really keeps his cool, thought Morgan. *Maybe that's what people mean when they talk about star quality. Being strong and calm—and hanging tough.*

"I'll do that," said Isis, her eyes flashing. "And don't be surprised if I'm not around when you get back." Her lip curled. "Not that you'd mind. I saw you and your new friend up on the pyramid. Pretty damn cozy."

With that, she turned and strode away.

"I'll go cool her down," Jonathan said. "Let's not break up the group over a little thing like this, guys."

He followed Isis toward a waiting limo.

"What about you, Willie?" said King. "You're the star of the next video. Got cold feet?"

Willie ran his hand through his silver-dyed hair. "I gotta say, this trip is getting *weird*."

King shrugged. "I can sit in for you—if that's how you want it."

Willie thought a moment. "Okay, I'll do it. I owe it to my fans, all five of them," he said with a grin. "Besides, it'll be a kick riding a horse. I haven't been on one since I was a kid at summer camp—before I got kicked out for playing drums over the P.A. system after lights out."

"What song is it for?" Sally asked King.

" 'Pale Rider,' " said King.

"With Willie on horseback?" said Jenny. "Wild."

"I hope the horse isn't," said Willie.

"Don't worry," said King. "Brian tells me it's a real pussycat."

A half hour later, when they arrived at the next site, Saqqara, where the oldest of the pyramids stood, Willie looked at the restless white stallion pawing the sand and said, "Some pussycat."

"I assure you, my friend, Moktar is gentle as a lamb," said the horse's owner, a small, dark-bearded man in Arab robes.

"Now it's a lamb," said Willie, who had changed into snow-white robes himself. "Funny, all I can see is a great big horse."

"Perhaps you would prefer another," said the owner, indicating a black stallion tethered nearby.

"Has to be white for the video," said Brian, patting the horse soothingly on its flank. "Don't worry, Willie, he's a sweetheart."

"Just don't rush us," said Willie. "I want Moktar to get used to me."

"Up you go," said Brian. "No time for you to form the basis of a lasting relationship."

As King, Morgan, and the girls tried to keep straight faces, Willie, with the help of the owner, managed to get up in the saddle.

Once up, he grinned. "Great. King, get set for a rival. I'm king of the desert."

"Don't get carried away," said Brian. "Moktar just has to go through the desert at a slow walk. We shoot you on horseback, then splice in shots of this pyramid here and the empty desert—to give the idea of 'Pale Rider'—that we're all small and frail and awkward as we go through life, surrounded by crumbling monuments of the past and moving through a world without roads or signposts."

"Hey, great interpretation," said King with a grin. "I didn't know I wrote such a *deep* song! You should toss away your camera and get a job as a rock critic, Brian. Or at the least write the liner notes."

"Scratch a director, and nine times out of ten you find an incurable intellectual," said Brian. "But come on now, let's get this show on the road."

He climbed into a jeep with a camera operator and motioned for Willie to get moving. But before he could, another jeep drove up. In it were Randy and Abdul, along with one of Abdul's men in the driver's seat.

"We've been scouting the territory around here, just to make sure there aren't any suspicious characters out in the desert," said Randy. "Can't be too careful."

"We are prepared to deal with any trouble," said Abdul, opening the jacket of his white suit to show a pistol in a shoulder holster. At the same time, the driver pointed to a submachine gun lying on the seat beside him. "Fortunately, we found nothing."

"Hey, maybe I should wear a pair of six-guns," said Willie. "Like, I'd be the Lone Pale

Rider, thundering out of the East."

"Come on, let's go," said Brian, glancing at his watch.

"Hi ho, Moktar," said Willie, and the horse began ambling gently over the sand. The jeep with Brian and the camera operator slowly circled him, getting shots from all angles as Willie headed out into the desert.

"I wouldn't mind a ride myself," said Morgan, eying the black stallion. It really was a magnificent animal. "It's been a while since I had a good horse under me."

"This animal is the very best—better even than Moktar," said the owner quickly. "And I am prepared to make you a very good rental price because I like you so much and you are such a very beautiful lady."

"How much?" asked Morgan.

"Twenty Egyptian pounds only—a price I would give to no other person in the world," said the owner.

"What about three pounds?" said Morgan.

"What an idea!" said the owner indignantly. "But because you have such lovely eyes, let us say fifteen."

"Because I am just a poor schoolteacher, let us say six," said Morgan.

"Because I admire the teaching profession, I will allow myself no profit after the expenses this magnificent horse inflicts upon me, and I will say twelve," said the owner.

"I will give up my dinner tonight and say

eight," said Morgan.

"I will match your sacrifice and take a loss. You can have the ride of your life for only ten," said the owner.

"Eight is as high as I can go," said Morgan.

"Impossible, dear lady," said the owner.

"Too bad. I guess I don't go riding," said Morgan with a shrug, walking away from the horse.

The owner shrugged resignedly. "Okay, eight."

Morgan was counting out the eight pounds when Sally said, "Look at Willie! He's gone crazy!"

"He really does think he's the Lone Ranger!" said Jenny as Willie's horse reared and then raced out into the desert with Willie hanging on for dear life.

"It's not Willie who's gone crazy—it's his horse," said Morgan.

As she spoke, she was already mounting the black stallion. The moment she was in the saddle, she gave the horse a sharp kick. It was only too happy to respond, and went after Willie like a shot. Morgan, despite the danger Willie was in, couldn't deny her exaltation at being on such a superb animal as it tore across the sand. This was what the horse had been bred to do—and what Morgan astride it felt like she had been born to do as well.

It took fifteen minutes at a gallop to catch up with Willie. By then he had dropped the reins and was clinging with both arms to the horse's mane, and his pale face had gone a sickly greenish-white. *Pale rider, indeed,* thought Morgan as she grabbed one of the flapping reins.

Turning the runaway horse in smaller and smaller circles, she gradually slowed it to a halt. Both horses stood side by side, their flanks heaving, as the two jeeps—one with Brian and the camera operator, the other with Randy and Abdul—reached them.

Randy and Abdul helped Willie down off his horse.

"Thanks," he said, standing on unsteady legs. "Think this monster is a member of the Egyptian Defense League? I do."

By now the owner had come riding up on another horse.

"I do not understand it, sirs," he said. "Never has Moktar done anything like this. Fortunately I have another animal who is absolutely guaranteed to cause no trouble. And because of this unfortunate incident, I will make you a very special price for him."

"No thanks," said Willie. "My days in the saddle are over. Get yourself another rider, Brian."

"Won't be necessary," said Brian. "I got enough shots to do the job—and actually, the shots we took of the horse running away might be used to good advantage. You know, for a kind of life-going-out-of-control effect."

"Too bad the horse didn't throw me and

trample me," said Willie. "That really would have packed a punch."

"Now that you mention it . . ." said Brian, with a speculative look in his eyes.

"Get me out of here," Willie said to Randy, "before the Marquis de Sade gets any more bright ideas."

The jeeps drove back to the starting point while Morgan and the horse owner on horseback walked the white stallion back.

King was waiting with a troubled expression on his face.

"Sorry, Willie," he said. "I'm beginning to think Jonathan and Isis are right. Maybe this trip is jinxed. Ever since we got to Egypt, I've had the feeling there are funny forces at work—almost like there are hostile spirits in the air. Maybe we shouldn't mess around here—it's ancient ground and we're exploiting it."

"King!" protested Randy. "This place has been exploited for thousands of years. The videos we're making here are nothing compared to what other people have grabbed."

"Absolutely," said Abdul. "In fact, the ancient Egyptians were the biggest tomb robbers of all."

Meanwhile Morgan, with Sally and Jenny beside her, was examining Moktar while the owner tried to persuade her to rent three horses so that Morgan and the girls could have a ride together. He promised them a very special group rate.

But riding wasn't what Morgan was interested in. A minute later, she found something that did interest her, and nodded to herself.

"Something wrong?" asked Sally.

"It seems so," said Morgan.

"With the horse?" asked Jenny.

"With the horse—and with this trip," said Morgan, her eyes serious. "The scene may be getting a little too heavy for you kids."

Morgan went to the minibus and returned with her shoulder bag. She took out her portable microscope and angled it so that she could use it as a looking glass to peer at a small swelling on the white stallion's rump.

"Bad news," she said to the others, who had gathered around her.

"What?" asked King.

"It wasn't a hostile spirit that entered this horse," said Morgan. "What put Willie's life in danger was very, very real."

Chapter 7

"I thought I saw a swelling on his flank," said Morgan. "Which made me suspect a puncture wound. When I magnified it, I found the wound. It's just a minuscule speck of dried blood. Somebody shot a dart into the horse to make it go out of control."

"But where is the dart?" asked Abdul, looking through Morgan's microscope.

"Probably it was made of a material that dissolved after it penetrated the flesh," Morgan said. "That way there would be no trace of any attack."

"Unless someone was as sharp-eyed as you, Miss Swift," said Abdul. "My compliments. You missed your calling. You would make a very good detective, I think."

Sally and Jenny exchanged glances. They knew from past adventures how good a detective Morgan Swift *did* make.

"Now we have to figure out who did it and why," said Morgan.

"A terrorist, I'm sure, and he doubtless used a blowgun," said Abdul. "They're easily imported from Africa and they do their job in silence. As for who it was, it could have been any of the people who rent horses and camels around here." He turned and looked at the man who had rented them their horses. "It could even have been you, my friend."

"*Me?*" the man said indignantly. "I swear by Allah . . ."

Abdul silenced him with a dismissive gesture. "I wish I had the power to search this man and all the others around here—but unfortunately I do not. And since it would not be to our interest to ask aid from the police if we want to keep the government from cutting short your stay in Egypt, the only thing we can do is to increase your security still further. I will hire additional personnel, if you agree."

"Get as many men as you need," said Randy, "no matter what it costs."

"I'll make your job of protecting us a little easier," said Willie. Though his ordeal was over, he was still paler than usual, which meant he was white as a sheet. "I've had enough. I'm grabbing the next plane back to the States. I'll see you all when you get back—if you get back. I hate to leave you in a hole, King, but I don't want to wind up in one myself. No hard feelings, huh?"

"No hard feelings—and no problem," said King. "We'll be able to do the rest of the videos without you. This last one was your big number—and it figures to come out fine."

"Thanks," said Willie. "I hate copping out, but I'm not the hero type. I'm into survival."

"You're not alone in that," said King. "I bet you'll have company on the flight home when

60

Isis hears about this."

But King was wrong.

When Isis learned of the fresh evidence of danger, she made it clear that there was one thing she feared more than the threat of death: the threat of not doing her big video number, scheduled to be shot the next day in Luxor.

"I just tried on my costume—it's a killer," she said.

"I'll say," agreed Jonathan. "If we had a few more videos of Isis, this album might not be such a disaster. Where are you going to shoot it?"

"In a tomb," said King.

Jonathan looked pained. "I was afraid you'd say something like that."

The whole group, including Randy, Abdul, Morgan and the girls, but minus Willie and Zack, were in Isis's luxurious suite. Isis had insisted on being moved into it when they had arrived at the hotel. She had asked the hotel manager where he ordinarily put visiting royalty, and told him that would do fine for her.

Willie, lightweight luggage in hand, was admitted inside by one of the two men guarding the door.

"I'm cutting out," he said. "There's a plane for New York in three hours—and they tell me it'll take that long to make it through traffic to the airport. I wish I could say I'm sorry to go, but I can't. Even this hotel is a bummer. I mean the service here. No one's changed the towels in the bathroom, and they haven't even picked up our breakfast tray from this morning. Zack left it in the hall and it's still there."

"Speaking of Zack, how is he?" Morgan asked Randy.

"Not so great," said Randy. "Like, he'll live, but he'll be real sick for a while. Seems he picked up a monster bug. The doc figured he bought some food on the streets or drank some nonbottled water."

"Don't know when he could have," said Willie. "I was with him most of the time, and anyway, Zack is real picky about what he eats. Actually, I was the crazy one, drinking water out of the tap and all."

"You're not the crazy one—King is," said Jonathan. "Look, King, there's still time to forget this whole idea, cut our losses, and pick up a bundle on a nationwide tour. I could set it up in no time—a solid concert with all your old hits. It would sell out every place we go."

"Don't listen to him, King," said Randy. "Remember, no pain, no gain. Gotta take chances to win big. Gotta go for it."

"I'm not into winning or losing—I'm not playing a game," said King. "I'm just doing what I have to." He spread his arms and stretched. "Right now I have to get some rest. Tomorrow's going to be a long, hard day."

With that, the group broke up. Willie took off for the airport, and the others left for their rooms.

"I'm starving," said Sally as she rode up the elevator with Jenny and Morgan.

"The hotel buffet dinner begins in an hour," said Morgan.

"I don't think I can wait that long," said Jenny. "I'm dying of thirst."

"We can order some Cokes from room service," said Sally.

"None for me," said Jenny. "I'm watching calories, starting today. Every time King looks at me I realize how tight my jeans are getting. And I don't think diet soda has reached Egypt yet. I'll just have some water."

"Get that from room service, too," said Morgan. "Bottled water. Remember what happened to Zack."

"Don't worry about that," said Jenny. "You know, I'm really surprised that a cool guy like Zack didn't watch out for the food and drink here."

"It is strange," agreed Morgan. She paused, looking thoughtful. "Look, you kids go to our suite by yourselves. Here's the key. I have a little errand to do."

Morgan got off the elevator on the floor below their suite, and the girls continued up. As soon as they were in their suite, Sally called room service. She ordered a Coke for herself, and a bottle of Perrier for Jenny. Just before she hung up she remembered to say that she wanted no ice in her Coke. Morgan had told her that bacteria in water could survive freezing.

"This is the life," Sally said, kicking off her sneakers and lying down on the bed. "Pick up the phone, get anything you want."

"Not bad," agreed Jenny. "I just hope the service isn't as bad as Willie said it was. That desert sun really did a number on me. I'm dehydrated."

Jenny didn't have to worry. In five minutes the door buzzer sounded.

An attendant was there with their drinks.

Sally gave him a small crumpled bill worth about ten cents as a tip and he thanked her profusely and left.

"The money in this country is strange," said Sally. "I haven't seen a coin yet. Everything is paper."

"People here must hoard any coins they get their hands on—they must figure the money isn't worth the paper it's printed on," said Jenny.

"Everything is so different from home," said Sally. "Look at our drinks. Back home they would have opened up the bottles for us. Here they leave them for us to open—I guess to reassure us that they're safe to drink."

"I'm opening mine right now," said Jenny, reaching for the bottle opener. At that moment the buzzer sounded again. Jenny opened the door to find Morgan, holding a tray loaded with glasses, bottles, plates, and serving dishes.

"You didn't have to bother—we already ordered by phone," Jenny said, and then saw that

64

the bottles and dishes on Morgan's tray were empty.

"You didn't drink any of that bottled water, did you?" Morgan asked anxiously.

"No. I was just getting ready to when you buzzed," said Jenny. "I'm parched."

"Look, share Sally's soda with her until I check something out," said Morgan. "On second thought, don't even do that. I'm afraid you'll have to suffer a little bit now—if you don't want to suffer a lot more later."

She set the tray down on a table. "It was lying in the hallway, just like Willie said," said Morgan. "I thought I'd have a look at whatever it was that Zack ate or drank."

"But how?" asked Sally. "They ate and drank everything. They must have been famished."

"But they didn't touch this," said Morgan, holding up an unopened bottle of water.

"What could be wrong with that?" asked Jenny. "It has to be safe. It's the same kind I have here—imported from France."

"Take a closer look at it," said Morgan, removing her microscope from her shoulder bag. She focused it on the bottle cap and let Jenny, then Sally, examine it.

"There are lots of little scratches on the side of the cap," said Jenny.

"A kind of wrinkle down its center," said Sally.

"Like it had been pried open," said Jenny.

"And then shoved back on," Sally completed

the thought.

"Not bad," said Morgan. "Now let's see what your bottle of water looks like."

She put the microscope on the bottle that Jenny had been about to open.

"The same marks," said Jenny.

"And your Coke, Sally," Morgan said, examining the unopened bottle, then handing it to Sally.

"More scratches," said Sally.

"Now let's find out what it all means," said Morgan.

From the portable chemistry kit in her shoulder bag she took transparent slides and an eyedropper. She labeled the bottle of water she had taken from Zack's tray to make sure she didn't confuse it with Jenny's bottle. Then she opened the labeled bottle and used the eyedropper to put a drop of water on a slide, and put it under the microscope.

"Look at those frisky little things," she said. "They must have a ball when they get inside you."

Jenny, then Sally, took a look at the multitude of organisms wiggling in the water.

"Yuck," said Sally.

"Are they dangerous?" asked Jenny.

"They could be," said Morgan. "Microbes like these aren't exactly your best friends. You saw how sick they made Zack, and he's a tall man with a strong build."

Morgan cleaned the eyedropper in a sterile

solution, then took a sample of water from Jenny's bottle and examined it. "More of the same," she said.

"I don't want to look," said Jenny, looking queasy. "What a close call."

Next Morgan examined the Coke. "Mmmm," she said, after taking a look. "I wonder if these bugs like the new Coke as much as they like the classic kind."

"Funny, I'm not thirsty anymore," said Jenny.

"Neither am I," said Sally. "In fact, I don't think I'll have anything to drink until I get out of Egypt."

"That was the idea—to get you out of Egypt," said Morgan. "You and Jenny and Zack and Willie. I'm sure I'm on the list, too, and everybody else in our group. Good thing Willie was crazy enough to drink tap water instead of the bottled water, or we wouldn't have had a clue as to what was causing the sickness. In fact, we all would have gone out of our way to drink this 'safe' bottled water."

"That Egyptian Defense League has some real shrewd operators," said Jenny.

"If it was the Egyptian Defense League," said Morgan.

"You don't think it was?" said Sally.

"There's only one thing I'm sure of at this point," said Morgan. "Whoever our enemies are, they're as hard to spot as these microbes— and as dangerous."

Chapter 8

Abdul Hakim went right into action as soon as Morgan told him about the doctored bottles. But an hour later, he had to admit failure. He couldn't catch whoever had done it. All he could do was say how it had been done.

"It was a highly professional job," he told the group assembled in King's suite. "They managed to divert your room service phone lines to a receiver they had set up in the basement. Then they sent up one of their men dressed as a member of the hotel staff. We found the receiver, and learned from some real staff members that they had seen this imposter. He told them he had just been hired, and they had no reason to doubt him. There is always a big turnover in personnel in a hotel as large as this."

"All I can say is, I'm glad I brought my own Perrier with me," said Isis. "You all laughed when I insisted on taking a case of it, but I knew better than to trust anything you get in a weird country like this."

"I guess they didn't figure out a way to spike my beer," said Jonathan Swine. "Or maybe the bugs are too small to attack somebody as, er, substantial as me. Anyway, I feel fine."

"So do I," said Brian. "Perhaps the terrorists

didn't consider me a proper member of the group, just one of the crew."

"I'm okay too—except for being shook up," King said. "I mean, I feel bad. I'm the one who got you all into this. Now Zack's in the hospital, Willie could have got his neck broken, and the rest of you have a right to be scared. Maybe I *was* doing a self-centered superstar bit when I insisted on this trip."

"That's what I've been telling you," said Jonathan.

"Like your brother's taking the count knocked you off balance," said Isis. "That's cool—for then. But that was months ago, King. It's time for you to get back in the groove, to the way you used to be. Time for *us* to go back the way *we* used to be—before you got the call about your brother and got into all this weird heavy stuff." Isis put one hand, its long nails painted icy silver, on King's arm. "Gotta get your kicks in the present, baby, 'cause that's all there is. Gotta forget about your brother."

It was exactly the wrong thing for her to say.

King stepped back. "He's the reason I wanted to do this album, and he's the reason I'm going to do it. I'm not doing it for money. Or for the fans. I'm doing it for him." King's voice softened, but there was no mistaking the resolve in it. "My brother wasn't here for very long, you know. And when he went, he went so fast. Like that." King snapped his fingers. "I want these songs to *last*."

"If *you* can last long enough to do it," said Isis, all sweetness gone.

"Sure he can—with Abdul's help," said Randy, his eyes glowing. "This is no time to chicken out. We're right on the brink of making something *big*. It'll go off the charts and into the stratosphere—I can feel those platinum vibes already. I've told Abdul to spend all the dough he needs to give us the cover we need, and he says we'll be as safe as if we were in the Palladium. Right, Abdul?"

"I don't know about this Palladium of yours, but you will be safe—if you follow my instructions," said Abdul in a take-charge voice. "I am chartering a private plane to take us to Luxor. The terrorists will not know when we intend to leave here and arrive there, and I have hand-picked the crew."

"When do we leave?" asked King.

"The sooner the better," said Isis. "The minute I finish my big number in Luxor, it's bye-bye to this creepy place for me."

"I thought you had *two* numbers in Luxor," said Randy.

"Brian says he doesn't need me for the second one," Isis said. "He's intercutting studio shots of me with some kind of tomb paintings." Her nose wrinkled in disgust. "Sounds really appealing," she said sarcastically. "I wonder how many mummies have TV sets."

Abdul looked at his watch. "Time to pack. We leave for Luxor in an hour. If we move fast, we will keep one step ahead of the terrorists."

"Look, could I have just five minutes alone with Sally and Jenny?" said Morgan, who had been following the conversation quietly and thinking hard.

"Sure," King said instantly. "Take as long as you want. I'm pretty sure I know what you want to talk about, and I don't blame you. This isn't kid stuff we've gotten into."

Sally and Jenny knew what Morgan wanted to talk about too. And they were ready for her.

As soon as they regrouped in the hotel corridor, Sally said, "I know, you want to take us back home now—to be safe."

"You figure it's your responsibility to our parents and all," said Jenny.

"But you're forgetting one thing," said Sally.

"What's that?" asked Morgan, half-amused at Sally and Jenny picking up the ball and running with it—and half-puzzled at where they were heading.

"King," Sally answered.

"King?" Morgan said.

"We could cut out and be safe—but what about him?" said Jenny.

"No one really wants to get us—but he's a natural target," said Sally. "He needs all the help he can get."

"He needs *your* help—unless of course you don't care what happens to him," said Jenny.

"Or unless you want to cop out and say that Abdul can do the job—after he hasn't been able

71

to stop any of the other stuff from happening," said Sally.

All this came out in a rush. Then the two girls paused for breath—and looked hard at Morgan, as if daring her to say she didn't care anything about King, or that she thought he would be as safe with her gone as he would with her around.

All Morgan could say was, "I suppose you two are right about not being on any primary hit list."

And, "King *is* in danger, no doubt about it."

And, "I do have some funny feelings about the people around him. Nothing definite. But *some*thing isn't right. I don't totally buy this terrorist business. It's too easy today to blame everything on terrorists—and too easy to get away with murder by doing it."

She didn't have to say anything more. Sally and Jenny said it for her.

"Then we're going to Luxor," said Sally.

"I knew we would all the time," said Jenny.

"Then you must have psychic gifts—very handy," said Morgan, smiling. Then she grew serious. "But if I'm going to be keeping my eye on King, you have to promise to keep extra alert and not expose yourselves to any risk—big or small."

Both girls nodded energetically in agreement. Though they tried to look serious, they couldn't keep from grinning as they followed Morgan back to join the others.

King smiled, too, when he heard the news.

"Great. I really would have missed you."

"Good. We don't have time to waste on good-byes," said Abdul. "We must move fast now."

There was no moving fast through Cairo traffic, though. The trip was made even more uncomfortable by the extra guards—big, burly men in cheap suits—who crowded into the minibus.

The plane waiting for them was far from uncomfortable. A sleek modern jet complete with wide leather lounge seats and a bar, it was pure luxury.

"It belongs to an oil sheik," said Abdul. "With the drop in oil prices, he's started renting it—discreetly. Not that he is inconvenienced. He has four more like it."

"There's even diet soda," said Jenny, looking at the beverage selection behind the bar. She reached for a bottle, then hesitated.

"Don't worry, everything on this plane is safe," Abdul assured her. "The ice included. And as soon as we take off, we will be served a most excellent dinner."

"Hey, dig the champagne," Isis said happily. "This baby is going to *bathe* in it."

"Talk about lifestyles of the rich and famous," said Sally as they all grabbed their favorite drinks. "Those ancient kings may have had great places for when they died, but you can't beat nowadays for living the good life."

"Don't be too sure about that," said Brian with a knowing smile. "Wait till you see what

73

we're shooting tomorrow morning."

The next morning, in the hour before dawn, Brian set the scene for them.

The whole group was on a ferry boat moving across the Nile. They stood on deck, bundled up against the chill, as the huge sky above them slowly brightened and the broad river changed from black to rippling purple.

Behind them on the east bank of the river was the town of Luxor. Ahead of them, on the west bank, they could begin to make out the shapes of hills in the distance.

"The kings moved their capital here from the area of Cairo after the time of the pyramid builders," said Brian. "Luxor was called Thebes then. On the east bank were palaces and temples. But on the west bank, where we're going now, there was only desert cut by deep valleys. It was good for only one thing, and the Egyptians made the most of it. Tombs."

"They got tired of building pyramids, huh?" said Isis. "It figures. They're not into hard work around here. The service is the pits."

"Not really," said Brian. "It's just that they were looking for better protection for their remains. Already the great pyramids had been looted. The rulers decided that a better way to assure their afterlives was to cut elaborate tombs into the sides of the valleys and conceal the entrances. Even inside the tombs, they built false walls to hide the resting places of their mummies. And of course they wrote threats of vengeance on all the walls for anyone who broke in. Not that it worked. Every tomb eventually was robbed—including the last one that was discovered, just sixty years ago. The tomb of the boy king, King Tut. His treasures are on display in the Cairo Museum. It was all legal according to modern law, but I'm sure his Ka feels it was just another robbery."

By now the boat was docking on the west bank. Waiting was a bus to take them to the Valley of the Nobles, where Isis was scheduled to perform.

"I can't believe you want me to dance in a *tomb*," she grumbled as the bus rolled down a dusty road. She shivered in her full-length fur coat. "The lights on me better be *hot*, Brian. Otherwise I'll have goose bumps on every beautiful inch of me—definitely not a turn-on for my fans."

"I'm sure you'll work up a sweat once you get going," said Brian.

"The only sweat I figure to have is a cold one," said Isis. "A tomb. Brrrr."

"Wait till you see it," said Brian.

The bus pulled off the road at a village of mud huts. Another bus was already there. It had carried the camera crew to set up the lighting in the cliffside tomb.

"It belonged to a wealthy aristocrat," Brian said as they followed a dirt path leading upward. Accompanying them was a swarm of barefoot children who had appeared as if by magic from the sleepy village. All offered to serve as guides in English at the top of their lungs.

Brian waved them off and continued with *his* guided tour. "Not being a king, he didn't have to fill his tomb with pictures of official ceremonies. He could picture the way he and his wife really lived—and how they wanted to keep on living after death."

When they entered the tomb through the narrow entrance, Isis took one look at the pictures on the walls and said, "Hey, not bad. I could make this scene myself."

"It looks like it was painted yesterday," said Jenny.

"They sure did know how to live," said Sally.

"And how to leave behind something after they died," said King.

Morgan simply said, "Extraordinary," as she took in the pictures covering the walls of the spacious room.

The brightly colored, beautifully drawn pictures showed an exquisitely handsome man and a beautiful woman enjoying all the pleasures of life—sailing in a gorgeous boat, feasting in a lavishly decorated room, hunting deep in a forest, being attended by countless smiling servants all the while. They seemed ready to step off the walls and into the room to continue their round of pleasures that very moment. For a moment, thousands of years vanished, and the people on the walls seemed to live again.

"I take back what I said, Brian," said Isis. "This will do fine for my number. Except do me a favor. Don't focus in on that chick on the wall. She's competition."

Isis took off her fur coat and handed it to Jonathan. Underneath she had on a belly dancer's costume—complete with a very wide bare midriff and a very filmy split skirt. While everyone else moved off-camera into a tunnel passage leading away from the painted room, Isis did a few stretching exercises, then said, "Okay."

"*Go*," said Brian. The camera began whirring, a tape began playing, and Iris began gyrating to:

> *"Money,*
> *how I want money,*
> *honey,*
> *how I want money,*
> *honey, money,*
> *money, honey,*
> *honey money*
> *sweet sweet*
> *sweet sweet*
> *heart*
>
> *Money,*
> *how you need money,*
> *funny,*
> *how you need money,*
> *funny, money,*
> *money, funny,*
> *funny money*

money funny
dear dear
dear dear
heart

Yes, the best things in life
cost a lot,
cost a lot,
Yes, the best things in love
cost a lot . . ."

Isis danced faster and faster, swung her hips harder and harder as the sound grew louder and louder and the beat quicker and quicker. When the number ended, she leaned limply against a wall, panting.

"Great," said Brian. "No need for a retake."

"Baby, it was *you*," said Jonathan, hurrying over to help Isis back on with her coat. "Straight from the heart. It had *soul*."

"Heart and soul's not what my fans dig," said Isis, looking down with satisfaction at herself in her skimpy costume before she put her fur back on. "I got more important assets."

"Baby, do you ever. I mean, you've got *every-thing*," said Jonathan, his voice oozing sincerity.

"Are you sure you're not saying that just because . . ." Isis said. She smiled coyly. "Should we tell them?"

"The news is too good to keep to ourselves," said Jonathan. His body seemed to swell with pride like a blimp about to burst as he turned to the others and made his announcement. "Isis has decided to become a star on her own, and I'm going to handle her career. She is also about to become a wife, and I'm handling that, too—as her husband."

"I hate to leave the group—but a girl has to look out for herself. I can't see any future for myself with Sphinx—not since King has developed so many other *in*terests, and I don't just mean his nutty new songs." Isis paused, shot a meaningful glance at Morgan, then looked directly at King. But if she expected him to argue, she was disappointed. He merely nodded.

Isis gave him, and then Morgan, a swift venomous glare. "I can see I was right," she said. "I wish I could say this last album has been fun, but why kid anybody? Jonathan and I are cutting out of this scene as soon as we can get back to the hotel and get packed."

Morgan and King exchanged glances and half-smiles. Isis hadn't wasted any time in looking out for number one. She must have been working overtime on Jonathan, who was looking at her with adoring eyes.

Jonathan put his arm around her and said, "You can leave your fox coat here in Egypt, baby. It's mink from now on. Stick with me. We're going places."

"I'm afraid you're wrong about that," said Abdul, stepping forward with two of his men. "The only place you two are going is jail."

Chapter 9

"I was hoping to give you two more rope to hang yourselves," said Abdul. "I had you under close surveillance, waiting for you to contact your confederates. But since you are not giving me that opportunity, I will take you into custody now, before you make your escape. I will make do with the evidence I already have—here."

Abdul pulled a telex from his pocket while his men pulled revolvers from their holsters and leveled them at Isis and Jonathan.

"Miss Swift," said Abdul, handing her the telex, "perhaps you would like to read this to the others. It was addressed to you."

"Then what are you doing with it?" asked Morgan. She did not like other people reading her mail.

"I apologize—but you must understand my position," said Abdul. "To provide security for The Sphinx, I must consider everyone a possible suspect—even you, Miss Swift. I made arrangements with the hotel to intercept all communications made to anyone associated with the group. This telex arrived for you yesterday."

"Then why didn't you let me see it after you read it?" asked Morgan.

"I did not want to risk your revealing its contents and alerting the suspects," said Abdul. "Read it, and you will see what I mean."

"Read it aloud," said King. "This proof better be good. Isis and Jonathan pulling heavy stuff? I don't go for it."

The telex came from New York.

" 'Dear Morgan,' " she read, " 'I tried to phone you at your hotel, but you were out, so I'm sending you this telegram. We found the person who put the threatening note in the food delivered to your New York hotel room. He told us the organization he worked for—a so-called export-import company that's really a gang of international criminals-for-hire. We got one of them to reveal who hired them to threaten The Sphinx. Two people—Jonathan Swine and Isis. The crime isn't serious enough to let us have them sent back from Egypt, but I'm sure you will know the right people to alert over there. Call me if you need help. Your man in blue, Patrick O'Connor.' "

"I think the evidence is convincing," said Abdul with a grim smile. He turned to Isis and Jonathan. "Want to save us a lot of trouble and confess? I warn you the Egyptian police are not gentle when they question suspects."

"We didn't mean anything *bad,* you got to believe us," said Jonathan. Sweat was pouring down his face, but he did not bother to mop it with his handkerchief.

"We were thinking of everybody's *good,*" said

Isis, who had gone deathly pale under her makeup.

"We didn't want to hurt the group—we wanted to stop it from getting hurt," said Jonathan, talking fast. "This *Death Trip* album is just that—a one-way trip to nowhere. We figured if we threw a little sand in the works, we could get the whole thing called off and get The Sphinx back on the right track."

"We could make everything like it was before," said Isis. She looked at King beseechingly.

"Poisoning Zack and almost killing Willie—you call that 'throwing a little sand in the works'?" said King, his face hard.

"The people I hired swore that the stuff they put in the drinks would just make someone a little sick for a few days—like lots of people get in Egypt anyway," said Jonathan. "And when Willie didn't drink the stuff, we arranged to get him thrown from that horse just to shake him up a little. Shake him up enough to do what he wound up doing and what we all should do—go back home where we all belong."

"Where you belong is in prison," said Abdul. "And I will make sure you go there."

"If anyone should go to jail, it's King," said Jonathan, losing control and flushing with rage. "He's the one who wouldn't listen to reason. He's the one who made us do this. What he's doing to the group is criminal. We were just acting in self-defense."

"What was I supposed to do—sit back and let

82

my image be put in the shredder?" demanded
Isis. "Nobody, but nobody, was going to kill my
career—not without a fight."

"Save your speeches for the judge," said
Abdul with contempt.

"No chance for us there," said Jonathan bitterly. "Nobody outside the business can understand all the sweat it takes to make it big, and
how easy it is see it all go down the drain."

"King knows, though," said Isis, looking him
in the eyes. "Unless he's forgotten all we went
through together, all we once were to each
other."

King's gaze stayed locked with hers a moment. Then, almost as if against his will, he
nodded. "I know, I know," he said. "Maybe I
should have done this alone. Maybe I shouldn't
have involved the group."

"But you did," said Isis bitterly.

"And now you've destroyed the group," said
Jonathan.

"And you've destroyed *us*," said Isis.

King sighed. "Okay, you guys win."

"You mean you're calling off the trip?" said
Jonathan, hope flashing in his eyes.

"And we all can get back together?" said Isis,
color returning to her cheeks.

"I mean you two can go off together," said
King. "Pack up and get out."

"But you can't leave crime unpunished," protested Abdul.

"Ever hear of karma?" said King.

"No," said Abdul.

"I didn't figure you did," said King. "You tell him what it is, Morgan."

"How do you know I know?" said Morgan.

"Just a hunch," said King, looking at her and smiling. "Am I right?"

Morgan nodded. "Karma is the idea that good breeds good, evil breeds evil," said Morgan. "And the only way to break the chain of evil is to return good for evil. That's what King's doing."

"I don't know about karma," said Jonathan. "But I do know that I owe you a lot for this, King. Thanks."

"I always knew you were a good guy," said Isis. "Thanks, too." She gave him a final, regretful look, then turned to Jonathan. "Let's get out of here."

"Before we go, I want to tell you something, King," said Jonathan. "One thing we didn't do was that terrorist threat against Morgan and the kids. That one was for real. Be careful."

"Thanks, Jonathan," said King.

"Good breeds good," Morgan said very softly.

"Come on, let's move it—if you *can* with all that weight you carry. Believe me, first thing after we're married, I'm putting you on a diet," said Isis to Jonathan. "And do me a favor, don't spend an hour haggling about the fare with the taxi driver. Spend a little dough for a change."

"We have to watch expenses until you're fully launched on a solo career," protested Jonathan.

"Next you'll tell me we can't go first class

back to the States," said Isis. "Loosen up, tight-wad."

They were still wrangling as they left the tomb.

"You know, I think their marriage to each other is going to be punishment enough," said King.

"More karma," said Morgan with a grin.

"Good thing we've already got a studio tape of Isis for the next video—and we've got her under contract, so we can use it," said Randy. Then he said, his voice intense, "We're gonna get these videos done, no matter what. Let's move it, Brian."

"What's the next stop?" asked Sally.

"I hate to tell you," said Brian. "It's another tomb."

"That's fine with me," said Jenny. "I never thought I'd say it, but I'm kind of getting into tombs. I mean, in Egypt it's like everything in them is alive."

On the bus, Brian told them about the next tomb.

"It belonged to Queen Nefertari, wife of King Ramses II," he said. "She was something special—a real beauty. And her tomb is something special, too. The portraits of her on the wall are the finest in Egypt. Wait until you see them."

"Hey, what are those huge statues out there?" asked Sally, looking out the bus window. They were passing three identical colossal statues of a royal figure, with the toppled ruins of a fourth statue lying on the ground.

"Statues of her husband, Ramses," said Brian. "He put statues of himself all over Egypt. As a matter of fact, we've already shot these to use in King's last big number, the one we're shooting at Abu Simbel. That's Ramses' big temple on the edge of the Sudan. That, thank God, will wind up this trip. I'll be happy to get this over and done with and get out of Egypt in one piece, I can tell you. So will my camera crew. It was all I could do to keep them from quitting the other day. There are easier ways for them to make a living than playing games with terrorists."

By now the bus had pulled up in front of Queen Nefertari's tomb. Brian had to show the guard even more documents than usual before he and the camera crew could enter and set up the lights while the others waited outside.

Then he went into the tomb and turned on a tape. It was Isis singing her last song, "Queen of the Scene."

"Weird, huh?" said Sally.

"Spooky," agreed Jenny. "Like hearing her ghost."

"Let's just think of it as her Ka—looking for a place to live again in this video," said Morgan.

The crew came out of the tomb for a break, and Brian followed. "You can enter now," he said. "Brace yourself for a stupendous sight."

"You first," said King to Morgan and the girls, waving them ahead.

As they entered, they could hear the words of Isis's song:

> "Gotta rock,
> gotta roll,
> but gotta stay
> in control.
>
> Set the beat
> with my feet,
> make the scene
> like a queen. . . ."

But the song faded from their consciousness when they saw the paintings of Nefertari that covered the walls.

"Do you see what I see?" said Jenny.

"Un*real*," said Sally.

They both turned toward Morgan. The face of Queen Nefertari was familiar—startlingly familiar.

If you changed her elaborate hair style into a short, punklike cut and put a streak of silver in it . . . If you exchanged her royal robes for a faded denim jacket, black cotton trousers, and red leather boots . . . you would be looking at Morgan Swift's perfect twin.

Both Sally and Jenny started to ask Morgan if she agreed, but they stopped when they saw her standing strangely quiet, gazing into empty air, as if half-stunned by the sight. The girls kept quiet, too, to give her space to recover her balance, collect her thoughts. Besides, their question was answered. They could be sure that Morgan saw what they had.

They were wrong.

Morgan was seeing far more.

She was seeing Nefertari, but not the painted image on the wall. Nefertari was emerging from a tunnel at the far end of the tomb—the tunnel to the secret spot where Nefertari's mummy had been hidden and later looted. Nefertari was coming closer and closer to Morgan until they stood face to face, and it was as if Morgan was looking into a mirror. Nefertari smiled then, a smile meant to still any fears Morgan might have, and then Morgan felt a quick, icy chill, and then a soothing warmth spreading through her. She was slipping into what felt like a delicious dream, and she could not stop it, did not want to stop it. A whole new world was opening up—

Then, with jarring suddenness, the dream was shattered—by the echoing crack of a rifle and a scream of pain.

Chapter 10

Morgan's body reacted even before her mind cleared. She raced to the entrance of the tomb, with Jenny and Sally behind her. She paused at the entrance and peered out, every sense alert.

But the danger had already passed. King, Randy, Abdul, Brian, and the camera crew were gathered around a groaning man lying on the ground. As Morgan approached, she saw that a trouser leg of the injured man was stained with blood.

"Just a flesh wound, fortunately," said Abdul, standing up after examining it. "No arteries hit."

"A sniper was on the top of the cliff," said Brian. "He winged Hank and then fled."

"My men are hunting him," said Abdul. "But I do not think their chances are good. He doubtless had a fast means of escape handy."

One of the camera crew said, "Well, we've got a means of escape handy, too. The plane. I'm speaking for all of us. We took a vote yesterday. One more incident, and we'd quit. That's what we're doing now."

The other men muttered their agreement.

"But I assure you, we will redouble our security," said Abdul.

"That's what you said last time," said another of the men. "We're getting Hank to the hospital—and then getting ourselves out of range of those nuts. The first plane out of here, man."

Brian shrugged. "I guess I could argue—but I won't. You have a right to worry—and look out for yourselves. Take the bus to transport Hank. I saw taxis down the road waiting to pick up tourists at the other tombs. We can use them to get ourselves back to the hotel."

Even Randy didn't argue with the crew. It was as if the shooting had sent him into shock. He merely said in a dead voice, "Tell the hospital to bill Megacorp. We're covered by insurance. It cost a bundle—and now I can see why." He shook his head and stared into space, away from the departing crew.

The crew helped Hank onto the bus. Then they went back to the tomb to get the equipment. They said they'd return it all to the hotel after Hank was taken care of. Two of Abdul's men went on the bus with them, in case they ran into trouble.

The bus rolled away, and what was left of the group—King, Randy, Abdul, Morgan, and the girls, along with three of Abdul's men—started down the road toward the taxis.

"There goes my big number at Abu Simbel," said King. "Seems a shame after we got this far."

"It is a shame," agreed Brian. "Abu Simbel is a choice spot. We could have capped off the series with a super video. I could hear your song in my mind as soon as I saw the place."

"You're not giving *up*?" said Randy. It was as if an alarm clock had gone off, waking him from a cat nap.

"No crew, no go," said Brian.

"Come *on*," said Randy, his voice jumping up in pitch, almost breaking like a teenager's. "We can't give up. We've come this far. All we need is this one last video to make the biggest hit of the year. We can do it. *You* can do it, Brian, baby. You know as much about lighting as those jerks who quit, and you can handle the camera yourself. All you need are some peons to do the lifting and hauling, and Abdul can supply them."

"The union wouldn't exactly approve," said Brian, shaking his head.

"Union, shmunion," said Randy, his voice practically setting off sparks. "This is *Egypt,* baby. I spread a few bucks around, and nobody says boo. Believe me, I know what I'm talking about. A little long green can go a long, long way."

Brian looked thoughtful. Then he shook his head again. "We don't have much time to shoot—and it would take too long if I had to oversee every move everyone makes. Besides, I need at least two cameras, to shoot different angles."

"I can't be*lieve* what you're telling me," said Randy, and there was genuine agony in his eyes. "There must be something we can do, some way . . ."

At that point, the same idea hit Jenny and Sally at the same time.

They turned to Morgan.

But before they had a chance to say what they were thinking, Morgan said it for them. "Look, I don't have a paid-up union card, but I once did some techie work for a rock group that came to San Francisco. I mean, that was years ago, but maybe I could help out."

"Don't let Morgan be so modest," said Jenny. "She once helped set up a Police concert."

"She even has a poster for it that Sting signed for her," said Sally, who had seen the poster on Morgan's wall.

"Can you handle a video camera too?" asked Brian.

"I've been fooling around with them a little this year," said Morgan.

"The more I see of you, the more you amaze me," said King, giving Morgan a look that Sally and Jenny would have died to receive.

The two girls exchanged glances. They mutely agreed that there was something going on between Morgan and King. A definite chemistry. Something interesting that might develop into something even more interesting.

"Morgan's like that," said Sally, to help the process along. "I mean, we've been her students for years, and she keeps amazing us more and more."

"Like in the tomb back there," said Jenny. "The resemblance between her and that Queen Nefertari was truly amazing."

"I didn't get a chance to see it," said King. "The rifle shot kept me from getting a good look. You say Morgan and Nefertari look alike?"

"Ask Morgan," said Sally. "She was looking at those pictures of Nefertari like she was seeing a twin."

"More like a ghost," said Jenny.

"The resemblance was strong," said Morgan.

"You're lucky the Ka of the queen wasn't hanging around," joked Jenny. "She'd have made a grab for you."

"Guess so," said Morgan, and quickly changed the subject. "Too bad we couldn't do the video in the tomb. There goes one of Isis's numbers. This wasn't her lucky day."

"We can always shoot that scene later—it doesn't require any members of the group," said King. "But maybe we won't bother. I wasn't too crazy about the song. We can give it to Isis as a farewell present—to use as a single."

"Let's forget about Isis," said Randy. "She's old news. Let's look forward to the final number—the climax to an album that's going to make history."

"I can hardly wait," said Sally. "I'll have a hard time sleeping tonight."

"You don't have to worry about that," said Brian. "There'll be no sleep for any of us tonight."

"Right," said King. "It's going to be a moon-light serenade."

The moon was full in a cloudless midnight sky as their bus rolled up to Abu Simbel. The last tourists were long gone, and now there was no one within miles, except the two guards who met their bus, checked their special papers, and turned on the lights that illuminated the temple entrances carved into the cliff.

"There are two temples—one for Ramses II and the other for Nefertari," Brian had explained on the ride from the airport. "They're wonders of the ancient world—and the modern world, too. Ramses had them carved into these cliffs to dominate the southern borders of his empire three thousand years ago. And less than twenty years ago modern technology moved these entire temples to higher cliffs when a lake formed by the new Aswan Dam threatened to destroy them."

Brian and Morgan, aided by Abdul's men, set up additional lights in front of Ramses' temple, while Jenny and Sally stared in awe at the gigantic statues flanking the temple entrance. Four colossal statues of Ramses seated on his throne—two on each side of the entrance —dominated the statue grouping. But there were also exquisitely fashioned statues of his wife Nefertari, his children, his ministers, and his soldiers, all much smaller than the king, but still much larger than human size.

"He was one powerful guy," said Sally.

"And he sure wanted the world to know it," said Jenny.

"Brian was right," said King. "This is the perfect spot for my song."

Brian and Morgan returned from setting up the lights.

"We're all set," said Brian. "Think you can manage that camera, Morgan?"

"Seems fine," said Morgan. "This new lightweight equipment makes things easy."

Brian ran through the shooting plan. King would be actually singing his song on camera, though his words and guitar music wouldn't be recorded here. He had already sung it in a studio back in the States, and that sound would be dubbed into the video. Brian, listening to the studio tape over earphones, would give King the beat to make sure he stayed in sync. As King sang in front of the temple, Brian would film him at an upward angle, so that he looked larger than life, just like the great statues of Ramses behind him. Meanwhile, Morgan would be filming him from up on the cliff, so that he would appear tinier and tinier as the song progressed. She would also get shots of the lake below the cliffs, with the moonlight forming a shimmering silver path on its rippling surface.

"I'm sure you two will do a great job," said King as he tuned his guitar. Brian and Morgan took up their positions. Jenny, Sally, Randy, and Abdul moved off to one side as King stood there, guitar in hands, dwarfed by the gigantic statues.

Then his voice rang out in the dead silence of the night:

> *"I am King*
> *when I sing . . .*
> *Yeah, I am King*
> *when I sing."*

Then it grew softer, more haunting:

> *"But the silence*
> *brings me down—*
> *that old silence*
> *brings me down."*

Once again his arrogant energy burst forth:

> *"I am King*
> *when I sing . . .*
> *Yeah, I am King*
> *when I sing."*

And again faded into a sound that was almost a sigh:

> *"The song is done*
> *and where's my crown?*
> *My song is done*
> *and where's my crown?"*

And finally, defiant and sad, he sang:

"So long, song,
so long, King,
gonna see
what the silence brings. . . ."

When it was over, King called down to Brian, "It go okay? I'll stay here all night if I have to."

"Perfect," Brian assured him.

"And the song is beautiful," came Morgan's voice from above.

"Great," agreed Sally.

"Sensational," Jenny chimed in.

"Well, that's the album," said King. "Done at last. Now we wait to find out what the public thinks."

"Before we pack up, are you sure you shot enough video?" Randy asked Brian.

"More than enough," said Brian. "All we have to do is edit it, and that'll be child's play."

"You're sure?" Randy persisted.

"Absolutely sure," said Brian.

"In that case, this death trip is about to come to a fitting climax," said Randy. He nodded to Abdul.

Suddenly there was a gun in Abdul's hand, and in the hands of the three men standing beside him.

"What's happening?" said King, voicing a question that was shared by Brian, Morgan, and the girls.

But there was no question about one thing.

The guns were pointed directly at them.

97

Chapter 11

"Hey, man, bad joke," said King.

"Believe me, baby, I wish it was a joke," said Randy, shaking his head. "But this is business, baby, business."

"Business?" said King.

"My business, baby," said Randy. "The record business. The business of this nutty album you're making. Maybe you got some kind of death wish—but I don't. If this album bombs, it blows me away with it. It was me who got Megacorp to put up big bucks, and it's me who pays for a flop. So I'm taking insurance. Death insurance. Your death."

"What are you raving about?" said King. He looked to Morgan for help. "Can you figure this guy out?"

"I'm afraid I can," said Morgan, realizing now what she should have realized all along. She should have realized that gleam in Randy's eyes was more than hyper energy or some kind of a permanent chemical high. She should have paid more attention to her vision of the vulture on the video screen in the Cairo hotel. She should have seen that the gleam in its eyes and Randy's eyes were the same—the ravenous gleam of a creature ready to feast on the dead.

"It seems Randy here has a certain lack of faith in *Death Trip*."

At this, Randy's boyish face twisted into a grimace of disgust. "Faith? What a laugh. I got faith all right—faith in what all those idiot fans are gonna do when they get a whiff of this junk of yours about life and death. They're gonna hold their noses and run. Un*less*," and a grin split Randy's face, "un*less* they hear about their idol King being knocked off by terrorists and leaving behind this album to all the fans he loved. You think John Lennon sales were good after he got his? That'll be peanuts compared to what *Death Trip* will do, especially after we finish with it. King, you're gonna become a martyred rock saint, and your last album is gonna be the biggest seller of all time. Of course, the other albums we put together out of *Death Trip* outtakes will clean up too. Before the public gets its fill, Megacorp will declare an extra dividend, and I'll have a big new title on my door."

"You're crazy if you think you can get away with this," said King.

"You're crazy if you think I can't," said Randy. "Or maybe crazy isn't the right word. Maybe dumb is."

"What about Brian, Morgan, the girls, the temple guards? They're all witnesses," said King. Then his face, tanned by the desert sun, went pale. "You don't figure to . . . you can't be that much of a . . ."

"I didn't get where I am in this business by being Mr. Nice Guy," said Randy. "Too bad about the schoolteacher and the kids, but you got to admit, I did my best to keep them from coming. They were just too thick to get the message. And then after Abdul's sniper got the camera crew out of the way, and Brian sprung that stuff about not being able to shoot this video alone, I couldn't stop Little Miss Swifty here from coming along to help. She and the kids should have done what the others did. They should have taken advantage of dumb luck when Jonathan and Isis saved me the trouble of having to get rid of the whole group. What a crazy slaughter that would have been. I got to admit, though, it might have sold a few more records. On the other hand, maybe we can have Isis and Willie and Zack do some kind of memorial album. Call it *Survivors* or something . . ."

King interrupted Randy's monologue. "I guess I don't have to ask about Abdul and his men."

"Abdul costs, but he's worth it," said Randy. "He and his goons will back me up on the story about a terrorist attack that wiped you all out. He'll even give me a little wound to make it more convincing. It pays to hire the best—especially when it's tax deductible."

"So it was you who planted that warning note from the Egyptian Defense League—to make this 'terrorist attack' more believable," said Morgan.

100

"Hey, you got brains, baby—too bad you didn't use them sooner," said Randy. "But as a matter of fact, you're wrong. That nutty note was just another piece of luck for me, like Jonathan and Isis's simpleminded scheme. It made all this easier." Randy grinned his boyish grin. "Hey, you know what I'm doing? I'm running off at the mouth, like one of those characters in mysteries who wastes so much time explaining how smart he's been that he loses his chance to kill the good guys. No way." He turned to Abdul. "Okay, Abdul. Remember, make it look good for the investigation later."

Abdul nodded. He and his men raised their guns.

King glared at them defiantly.

Brian bit hard on the unlit pipe in his mouth.

Sally and Jenny bit their lips hard to keep from crying. Desperately they looked at Morgan to see if she could do something, anything, to get them out of this.

But Morgan could only shake her head sadly. For once in her life she had to admit she had no idea what to do.

The two girls could only shut their eyes and wait for the gunshots.

They did not have long to wait.

Deafening explosions blasted their ears.

They waited for the pain.

There was none.

Had they been killed instantly? Was this what death was like?

Neither of them had the nerve to open her eyes to find out.

Then each of them felt a hand in hers, jerking her sharply into movement. At the same time they heard a voice, Morgan's voice, shouting, "Run!"

The girls strained to keep up with Morgan as she made a beeline out of the danger zone. Behind them, gunfire from unseen attackers in the dark and from Abdul and his men defending themselves was turning Abu Simbel into a gigantic shooting gallery.

"Keep up the pace!" Morgan gasped over her shoulder. "Another minute and we'll be—"

But she did not get to say "safe." Coming around a hill ahead of them were two men in Arab dress. They carried submachine guns.

All Morgan could say was "In here" as she darted into the mouth the temple built two hundred yards from the Temple of Ramses II.

"What is this place?" Sally's voice asked in the pitch darkness.

"The Temple of Nefertari, I think," Jenny said.

"We'll see if it is," said Morgan's voice. A moment later her flashlight cut through the darkness.

"It's the Temple of Nefertari, all right," Morgan said as she shone the flashlight on a wall painting of the queen. Again she found herself staring mesmerized at a face that was a mirror image.

The sound of guttural voices outside the temple entrance snapped her out of it.

"They saw us come in here," Morgan said to the girls. "They're probably figuring how best to come in after us. As soon as one of their pals arrives and tells them he saw us running away unarmed, they'll stop hesitating."

"But who *are* they?" asked Sally.

"Think about it a second—it'll come to you," said Morgan.

"I know," said Jenny. "The Egyptian Defense League."

"Right," said Morgan. "Randy forgot that there's a real world outside the rock world. And in that world there are real terrorists."

"What do you think they'll do to us?" said Sally.

"I don't want to know," said Morgan. "We have to find a way out of here."

Morgan turned the flashlight beam away from the face of Nefertari and saw three tunnellike entrances leading farther back into the temple.

"Eenie, meenie, minie, moe—let's go," she said, and led the girls through the tunnel on the left into another room, this one smaller than the first, but even more elaborately decorated.

"This is a traditional temple," said Morgan. "A series of rooms getting smaller and smaller until the final room where only the priests and royalty could go—the Sanctuary of the God." She played her light along the wall until it lit another tunnel entrance. "I have a hunch that this one goes there."

But Morgan hesitated at its entrance. "If there's no way out beyond this, we'll be caught like rats in a trap."

She heard voices from the room they had just left.

"They've figured out we're defenseless," she said. "They're probably trying to decide which tunnel to come through after us. They don't know that all three lead into this room. Let's go before they find out."

She led the girls into the next tunnel.

"I was right," she said when they emerged into the room beyond. "We're in the sanctuary."

Before them was a statue of Hathor, the Egyptian cow god, symbol of divine nourishment. On the walls were larger-than-life paintings of Ramses and Nefertari meeting with Hathor, making offerings to the god, and in return being granted godlike power.

But Morgan was interested in none of that. Desperately she played the flashlight around the room, looking for a way out.

The flashlight beam moved along the walls, then the floor. Nothing.

"No way out—and no more time," said Morgan. "There has to be *some*thing we can do."

In a final gesture of desperation Morgan shone her flashlight on the ceiling—and then wished that she hadn't.

There, painted on the ceiling, were giant vultures, looking down in hideous anticipation of the feast of death to come.

Chapter 12

Suddenly the sanctuary was lit by dim electric light.

The terrorists had found the switch to turn on the lights within the temple.

A voice came from outside the sanctuary. "We know you are in there and unarmed," it said in slightly accented but fluent English. "We will give you five minutes to come out peacefully, or we will come in after you. I advise you to avoid violence. Surrender, and we will not harm you."

"No way I believe him," said Jenny.

"I don't, either," said Sally. "What do you think, Morgan? Can we trust him?"

"I'd hate to bet my life on it—which is what we'd be doing," said Morgan. "Not that we have any choice."

Even as she said this she kept looking around the sanctuary, searching for something, anything, that she might have overlooked.

She saw nothing.

Then she saw—everything.

It happened when her eyes met the eyes of the painting of Nefertari—met them and were held by them.

Before her eyes she saw Nefertari move away

from the wall and toward her, just as that ghostly figure had in the tomb at Luxor.

Again she stood face to face with Nefertari—and felt the sudden chill, then the warmth spreading through her, as if she were slipping into a dream.

This time nothing interrupted it.

Morgan was still Morgan, but at the same time she was not. She was still standing in this sanctuary, but now it was lit with flickering torches, and the paintings on the wall were fresh and bright. She stood beside a tall and powerful king, who wore the double crown of Upper and Lower Egypt, decorated with the protective symbols of the north and south—the Cobra for the north, the Vulture for the south. The High Priest of the temple was showing them the secrets of the sanctuary, pressing the eye of the painting of the god Hathor. When he did this, a flawlessly concealed panel in one of the huge blocks of stone on the wall swung open, displaying a cache of objects wrapped in fine linen. He smiled, closed the panel again, and workers came to put the finishing touches on the secret compartment. They inserted tubes to suck out the air within and then sealed the vacuum they had created. No decay would ever affect the hidden objects, for these craftsmen built their works to last for all time, and they were masters.

Morgan knew all this without knowing how she knew it. She was thinking in a language she did not understand, yet which told her all. She was Morgan Swift and she was another who had joined with her—not to conquer her, but to tell her what she had to know. Morgan was moving through time now, seeing years of rituals in this sanctuary, then years of darkness, then figures in ancient dress breaking into the sanctuary, looting all precious objects and leaving it to many more years of darkness. Then others, pale-faced ones in European garb, entered and brought light with them. The years were speeding up now, and there were millions of curious tourist faces and the babble of countless guides talking in many tongues. Then there were engineers coming into the sanctuary, and giant machines and sweating laborers moving the building blocks to another site without discovering the secret compartment within, and then more tourists, more guides, and then—

Morgan was standing in front of the painting of Nefertari. She was shaking her head to clear it.

How long had her trance lasted? She looked at Sally and Jenny and saw that they had seen nothing unusual. Not more than a few seconds had passed, maybe not even that. She had stepped out of time to travel through thousands of years—and now time was running out unless she acted fast.

She thought fast. First of all, she did not want the girls to suspect where she had just been and what she had seen. Morgan preferred to keep her private powers to herself, rather than having to explain what she could not explain. She went to the wall on which the god Hathor was painted and hit it with her fist in what the girls would see as a display of frustration and desperation.

Her fist hit the eye of the god, and what Morgan was praying would happen did happen.

The panel in the wall swung open. There was a hissing sound as air entered the secret compartment for the first time in three thousand years.

Morgan took the barest minimum of time to look startled for the girls' benefit. Then she reached into the compartment and took out the linen-wrapped objects. Swiftly she peeled off the linen strips to expose what she somehow knew was within.

A beautifully fashioned bow, tautly strung. As the girls watched her wide-eyed, she unwrapped individual arrows—ten of them. After that, she unwrapped a knife and a spear.

She paused only to say "Incredible," before handing Jenny the knife and Sally the spear and whispering, "Stand on either side of the entrance. And get ready to move fast. No time for instructions. I know I can trust you to use these if it's a matter of life or death."

Then Morgan took the bow and arrows and stood against the wall behind the statue of Hathor facing the entrance. A voice sounded from the room outside.

"Your time is up. Coming out? Or do we

come in?''

Morgan shouted back, "I warn you, we're armed!''

"Don't try to bluff us—we know better," the voice said.

But the figure who came first through the entrance took the precaution of holding his machine gun ready.

It didn't do him any good.

An arrow caught him in the upper arm and he recoiled in pain, dropping his gun. He smashed directly into his companion who was close behind him, hitting the barrel of the second man's gun and turning it aside.

Before either man could recover, Morgan had advanced on them. Another arrow was in her bow, and it was pointed directly at them.

Meanwhile, Jenny's knife was at one man's throat, and the point of Sally's spear was on the other's.

The second man didn't have to be told to drop his weapon and raise his hands, and they both instantly followed Morgan's command as she gestured for them to enter the room. As they stood against the wall with their hands above their heads, Jenny and Sally scooped up the machine guns and brought them to Morgan.

"I know more about using a bow than one of these things," said Morgan, pointing one of the machine guns at the men. "But I guess I can't miss at this range."

From outside a voice yelled in Arabic.

"What's he saying?" Morgan asked her captives in a whisper. "Keep your voice down when you tell me."

The terrorists stared at the gun trained on them, and one of them quickly answered in a low voice, "He's asking if we've got you."

"Tell him you have," said Morgan. "Tell him to come in—and no tricks."

The man shouted in Arabic, and another man came through the entrance. The next moment, he was standing with his hands raised beside the other two.

"Any more of you outside?" said Morgan. "I don't advise you to lie."

"No. The others are busy taking care of your friends," said the first man. Then he added, "Be careful of the way you handle that gun of mine. It's hair-triggered. Very sensitive."

"So am I—to any signs of resistance," said Morgan. "When the girls tie you up, don't even think of pulling any funny business." She nodded at the girls. "Sally, Jenny, you can use those strips of linen the weapons were wrapped in."

"But my arm," said the man. He had managed to extract the arrow, but the wound was ugly.

"I'll take care of that in a minute," said Morgan.

After Jenny and Sally finished tying the men's hands behind them and tying their feet together, Morgan checked their work.

"Good job," she said. Then she took a first-aid

kit from her shoulder bag, applied antibacterial ointment to the man's wound, and bandaged it.

"That ought to hold up okay—until you can get better attention in a prison hospital," said Morgan. She turned to Sally and Jenny. "Each of you grab a gun. We'll see if we can help the others—if it isn't too late."

Both girls picked up machine guns and held them gingerly.

"I have no idea how to use one of these," Sally said.

"Me, either," said Jenny. "I was never big on playing with war toys."

"It doesn't matter," said Morgan. "The nice thing about impressive-looking weapons is that you don't have to use them. Nobody will want to test your skill. Come on."

Leaving the three terrorists tied up behind them, Morgan and the girls left the Temple of Nefertari. Morgan paused before the final exit. She peered out cautiously, then edged herself out, motioning for the girls to follow. Two hundred yards away, the other terrorists—six of them—were busy tying up King, Brian, Randy, Abdul and his men, and going through the loot they had gathered from their captives' pockets. Their victory had been complete.

"You think we can tackle them with guns we can't use?" whispered Jenny.

"We've got a much more effective weapon on our side—surprise," said Morgan. "Let's use it—before we lose it."

Moving swiftly along the side of the cliff, with the girls behind her, Morgan got within a hundred feet of the terrorists. Then she announced her presence with a gentle, quick squeeze of her trigger finger.

Bullets kicked up dust a few feet from the terrorists. They whirled around, grabbing for their guns, only to see Morgan and the girls moving straight toward them, machine guns trained on them at a distance that made resistance suicide.

The terrorists raised their hands in silence and quickly obeyed Morgan's orders to untie King, Brian, and the two temple guards who Morgan now saw were with them.

"What about us?" Randy said indignantly.

"Do you have to ask?" Morgan said.

Randy shrugged. "Guess not. Well, you win a few, you lose a few." He tried his boyish grin on her. "So tell me, Morgan, what kind of deal do you want to cut? You can make a mint."

"I'll be glad to talk about a deal," said Morgan. She smiled when she saw the startled looks from King, Brian, and the girls. "Let's have lunch—in five or ten years. You should be out of jail by then."

Chapter 13

"I'm sorry I can't stay to testify at the trial," Morgan told King at the Cairo airport two days later. "But the sworn statements the girls and I gave to the police should be enough, along with Brian's testimony and the temple guards' and yours."

"I wish you could stay, too," said King. "But not for the trial."

Jenny and Sally, standing off to one side, looked at each other. This was the moment they had been waiting for. They had seen the feeling between King and Morgan building and building. Now it was surely going to break through the surface.

Much as they badly wanted to be around to see it, they knew they had to give it space to happen.

"We've got some stuff we have to do by ourselves," said Jenny.

"Some last-minute shopping at the duty-free shop," said Sally. "I never got a chance to buy any henna or kohl—and they have the best in the world in Egypt."

But Morgan nixed the idea, saying it was too close to boarding time for the girls to be wandering off on their own.

It was almost as if Morgan was afraid to be alone with King, though the girls could hardly believe that. Being afraid of things wasn't Morgan's style. But still . . .

There was a definite uneasiness in the way Morgan returned King's intense gaze. A definite edginess in the way she responded to his close physical presence.

"Look, I want to see you again when I return to the States," said King.

"Sure. We'll get together—sometime," Morgan said with deliberate vagueness.

"I've never known anyone like you—and I'd like to get to know you better," King persisted.

At that moment, a voice came over the public address system: "Immediate boarding for Air Egypt flight 432 to New York. Passengers please go to departure gate twelve."

Something very close to relief showed on Morgan's face.

"Gotta be going now," she said quickly. "So long." Then, in a softer voice, she said, "We'll keep in touch."

Morgan and the girls left King standing there, a puzzled look on his face.

Sally and Jenny had puzzled looks on their faces too.

"Maybe I was wrong, but it looked to me like King was coming on real strong to you," Sally said to Morgan.

"Maybe too strong," said Morgan, not meeting Sally's inquiring eyes.

"What was the matter, didn't you *like* him?" asked Jenny incredulously.

"Sometimes you can like someone *too* much," said Morgan.

"You mean you're afraid a big star like King would just use you and drop you?" asked Sally. "King's not like that at all."

"He's okay," said Jenny. "He's *more* than okay. I can't see any reason anyone could *want* to turn him down."

"Maybe that's the trouble—maybe I can't either," said Morgan, and then she stopped abruptly, as if she had said too much.

Unable to evade the girls' questioning gazes, she added, "Let's just say I made a promise to someone once. A promise I don't want to break."

Both girls remembered the guy in Morgan's past, the guy who died, the guy Morgan would never talk about. They knew it was useless to ask her about him now.

The only question they could ask was the one that Sally did: "What will you do if King gets in touch with you?"

"That's a bridge I'll have to cross—or maybe I won't," said Morgan as they joined a crowd moving toward the bus that would take them to the plane on the runway. "King is going to be real busy from now on. First with the trial, then with the album. All the publicity is going to make it a huge hit—though I have a hunch it would have been one anyway. I think the next time I see King, it'll be on the video screen."

A week later, the girls had to admit that Morgan was right.

They were watching King on the video screen—the screen of Morgan's VCR.

Morgan had received the videotape in the mail—air express from Cairo. She asked the girls to come see it.

"Look familiar?" Morgan said as a series of vivid wall paintings flashed on the screen.

"It's the tomb of Nefertari," said Sally. "She looks as much like you as ever."

"It's the other way around—I look like her," said Morgan with a smile. "She's been around a lot longer than I have."

"But why does King want us to see Isis's number?" wondered Jenny.

Her question was answered when King appeared on the screen, doing a solo on his guitar, his voice and his sound more vibrant with raw emotion than ever before.

"He's doing a new song," Jenny said before she shut up to make sure she didn't miss a word.

> *"It's here today,*
> *gone tomorrow,*
> *no use to beg,*
> *nothing to borrow.*
>
> *Yeah, here today,*
> *gone tomorrow,*
> *no use to cry*
> *when you say good-bye.*

So fare you well
my black-haired queen,
the fairest girl
I've ever seen.

Oh, fare you well
my lovely one—
the only queen
I've ever known. . . ."

After the video ended—with a long closeup of Nefertari's face, the girls turned instantly to look at Morgan.

"Was there some kind of note with the video?" Jenny couldn't keep from asking.

"King have anything to say—besides all he said in that song?" Sally added.

"There was a note—a short one," said Morgan. Then, seeing that the girls didn't have the nerve to ask what they were clearly dying to find out, Morgan said, smiling, "It really doesn't say much. If you like, you can read it."

"We'd like," Sally said.

Morgan handed them a sheet of airmail paper. The girls held the translucent paper down on a tabletop so that they could read King's handwritten words:

Morgan, hi.
I've been doing some reading and found out that the Greeks believed in the Sphinx, too, but they believed it was a woman. After meeting

you, I have to agree. You're my Sphinx—and I'm bound and determined to solve your riddle someday.

Till then,

King

"Funny letter," Morgan mused.

But Sally and Jenny didn't think it was funny at all. For they, too, were bound and determined to solve the riddle of Morgan Swift . . . someday.